North Point of View:
Tales of Alpharetta and Beyond

To Lynette with thanks for all of your help. John Sheffield.
Roswell, Georgia, March, 1- 2010.

North Point of View:
Tales of Alpharetta and Beyond

A collection of Short Stories and Poems

by Multiple Authors

North Point Writers

iUniverse, Inc.

New York Lincoln Shanghai

North Point of View: Tales of Alpharetta and Beyond

iUniverse books may be ordered through booksellers or by contacting:

iUniverse
2021 Pine Lake Road, Suite 100
Lincoln, NE 68512
www.iuniverse.com
1-800-Authors (1-800-288-4677)

This is a work of fiction. All of the characters, names, incidents, organizations and dialogue in this novel are either the products of the author's imagination or are used fictitiously.

ISBN-13: 978-0-595-41535-9 (pbk)
ISBN-13: 978-0-595-85882-8 (ebk)
ISBN-10: 0-595-41535-0 (pbk)
ISBN-10: 0-595-85882-1 (ebk)

Printed in the United States of America

Contents

Contents

Contents

Foreword

A number of writers from North Atlanta meet on every second and fourth Saturday of the month at the North Point Barnes & Noble to critique each other's writing. Spurred on by our facilitator, Rob Elliott, we have produced an anthology of pieces relating to the Alpharetta-Roswell area. Our contributions, and those of a few invited contributors, cover the gamut of human emotions with essays, poems, short stories and nonfiction. We hope you will enjoy *North Point of View: Tales of Alpharetta and Beyond.*

Acknowledgments

The Alpharetta Barnes & Noble Writers Workshop is deeply appreciative of Barnes & Noble for providing a place for meetings and for offering technical advice. In particular, we thank former employee, Rob Elliott, for suggesting the anthology and providing continued encouragement up to the time he left to take a teaching job near Savannah. We miss him, his enthusiasm, and his knowledge of literature.

Bozo, Dog of the 'Hood

By Dagmar Marshall

The day my husband, Charlie, brought the English bulldog puppy home, I cracked into a million pieces. We'd raised four kids, outlived three dogs, two cats and a jumble of parakeets, hamsters and rabbits. I wanted no tie-downs. I wanted to kick back and enjoy an uncluttered, quiet house. I wanted an undemanding lifestyle.

Charlie cradled the poopy thing like it was a newborn baby. He introduced it to me like it was a real person. "Bozo, meet Mabel, the lady of the house. She's gonna love you just like I do."

"Charlie," I spoke through clenched teeth, "it just wet all over your best golf slacks."

"Mab, this pup is a blood relative of the current Uga but with all due respect to the legendary Georgia bulldog mascot, I've named him Bozo. Means a real guy."

"Bozo also means jerk."

Charlie frowned. "Hey, don't call Bozo a jerk. Me, maybe, but not an innocent pup." He held it up close to my ear. "Here, he wants to say hello." The dog took one lick, followed immediately by puppy teeth in my ear lobe.

"Charlie, get him out of here. Look, he nearly tore off my ear. I'm bleeding." I was also shrieking.

Charlie stepped back. "Mabel, he's sorry. I'm sorry. He's just a baby. Look, I've got a crate for him. I'll take him for walks and I'll feed him. Just leave him to me. This is really a big moment for me, Mabel." He snuggled the thing into his neck and grinned at me. "This is my own University of Georgia bull-dawg."

I was beyond speech. Charlie had clearly chosen a dog over me, his wife of thirty-five years. An ugly dog, at that.

"Charlie," I pleaded, "how about I'll sleep in the crate and you can walk and feed me? Then, we'll both be happy. I'll even wear red and black."

Charlie shrugged off my sorry attempt at humor. My husband's fierce loyalty to the University of Georgia football team and its famous mascot was matched only by his alumni friends in the neighborhood. I was convinced they would all bleed red and black if punctured. In fact, Charlie had begun to resemble an English bulldog. Round faced, stocky, and noticeably bowlegged. He denied that. But I can see, can't I? The man had taken on the physical appearance of the very dog he loved so much.

Charlie handed the pup to me while he dabbed at his peed-on slacks. Bozo promptly anointed my sweater. The dog looked at me with round, brown luminescent eyes that I swear were filled with laughter. I held him out at arm's length. "Damn, Charlie, take this thing."

Charlie cuddled Bozo back to his chest. "See ya later, Mabel. Bozo has to make the rounds and meet his fan club."

"Charlie, where's his leash?"

"Bozo doesn't need a leash. He's only two months old for God's sake. I'll probably have to carry him most of the time, anyway."

I swallowed. "Charlie, if you take that dog out of this house without a leash, you know what will happen."

Charlie pursed his lips. He squinted his eyes. He flapped his free hand, taunting me. "You can't mean we'll get a letter from The Board?"

"You're not funny and neither is The Board. I don't care if you carry the dog every minute of the way—put him on a leash."

Bozo yipped at me. I tried to stare him down. "And you, dog, don't you dare talk back to me. You *will* be on a leash." Bozo licked his chops and drooled. Fool thing was probably hoping for another bite of ear lobe.

It was a game day. The Fanatics, as I referred to the University of Georgia Bulldog Alumni of the Halyard Point Cluster Home Community, held a worship-of-game-day ceremony that would beat high mass in any church. All eight of them gathered at the previously determined First Quarter Home, then, on schedule, marched to the Second Quarter Home, then…you get it. No doubt, Bozo would be the blazing hit of every quarter and I would become the target of scalding repartee among the wives. "I can't believe Mabel let Charlie bring a two-month-old puppy into my home. The thing slobbered all over my couch and peed on the carpet. Mabel has lost her mind, and Charlie is an idiot."

I put the half-time hors d'oeuvres and cold beers on the screened porch and thanked the Lord that it was a warm day and I could keep the Fanatics and Bozo out of the house. They came in, tight-lipped and snarly. The Dawgs were losing. But Bozo cheered them by pooping on the carpet. This was determined to be a good omen. The Dog of Dawgs! His pug nose glistened and his big pink tongue dripped all over anyone who came close. They all picked him up and received either white dog hair on their clothes or a baptism of dog pee. Bozo was King.

Charlie and Bozo returned after the game. Dawgs won. I paid silent homage to the football gods. I could look forward to a week of a smiling, happy-go-lucky Charlie. Bozo dragged a greasy ham hock across the kitchen floor, a reward from the Fanatics, and flopped down in a corner to test his razor teeth.

A winning season saw Bozo elevated to idol-like stature. The Fanatics watched and cheered as Charlie and Bozo walked to each football house, every day, and left each yard a little worse for wear, every day. During the months of football, the mighty Bozo put on twenty pounds and now stood twelve inches at shoulder height. His head grew massive, and his already-wrinkled face crumpled into canyon-like folds.

Bozo slept in our room, on the floor beside Charlie, and he snored. A lion could take roar lessons from that dog. I finally stood up for myself. "Charlie, I love you. I don't love that dog. Now, he sleeps somewhere else, or I sleep somewhere else."

"Mabel, Bozo can't help it."

"That's it. You've made your choice, Charlie." I grabbed my favorite pillow, yanked the comforter off the bed and headed for the guest room. My foot hit something furry and growly. Bozo had positioned himself in front of the doorway and didn't like being kicked in the ribs.

"See, Mabel, he wants you to stay here with me. And I want you to stay here with me."

I didn't believe that Bozo wanted me to stay, not really. However, I did believe that Bozo knew that if I left the bedroom, it could be outsville for him.

I wimped. "Okay, I'll try ear plugs, but if that doesn't work..."

Charlie grabbed me in a gorilla hug and tossed me back onto the bed. Bozo grumbled, slobbered and took his place back beside Charlie, and commenced snoring. I put in my earplugs.

*   *   *   *

The next season began and Bozo now weighed in at fifty-five pounds and stood fourteen inches at the shoulder. "Taller than the average Dawg," Charlie bragged.

On opening day of the new season, the pride of the Halyard Point Cluster Home Community UGA Football Alumni discovered an unattended bowl of onion dip at the Third Quarter house and he promptly devoured it. The host of the Third Quarter house thought it was hilarious. The perfume of Bozo's breath combined with the aroma of gaseous expulsions of a bulldog who has just inhaled a bowl of onion dip, failed to amuse the hostess. Bozo was cast out from the Third Quarter house. To Charlie's delight, the floppy-jawed monster was waiting patiently for him at the Fourth Quarter house. "A dog of supernatural powers," he declared. The Fanatics applauded and cheered.

The Fanatics turned their heads to Charlie's flaunting of the leash law on Bulldog Days and all other days. The rest of the neighborhood did not. The scathing letters from The Board of Directors of the Halyard Point Cluster Home Community reminding us of the "leash law" were increasing at an alarming rate. Imminent and on-going fines were on the docket.

My voice hit high C. "Charlie, you've got to quit walking that dog without a leash. We're close to being totally ostracized because of Bozo. The alumni wives don't even wave at me anymore. You're slapping everyone in the face with your actions, Charlie, and I don't think it's funny. That dog," I pointed a finger at Bozo as he shook his massive head, flinging slobber everywhere, "could drown a baby in all that drool he throws around. If a child on a bike ran into him, there'd be broken bones followed by a big, fat lawsuit. Put him on a leash!"

Bozo looked up at me with total disdain flashing from his big brown eyes. I guessed at his Bulldog thoughts. They weren't nice.

*   *   *   *

Bozo now stood sixteen inches at his shoulder and according to Charlie, weighed in at fifty-eight pounds. It was agreed among the UGA Alumni of the Halyard Point Cluster Home Community that Bozo was the most magnificent and intelligent bulldog ever born. Too bad Bozo couldn't be the Uga of the games between the hedges, they chorused. I determined to call the University and volunteer Bozo for a lifetime Uga-substitute role.

The Fanatics were convinced that Bozo was the reason for another winning UGA football season. The Board and everyone else were convinced that Bozo was a nuisance and Charlie was the perpetrator of the internal fray that was exploding throughout the streets of the Halyard Point Cluster Home Community.

"Charlie, do you realize that this whole neighborhood is about to take up arms against each other because of Bozo? You simply must walk him on a leash. It would solve *everything*."

Charlie absently scratched Bozo's floppy ears. "Mab, it would destroy Bozo's macho image if he showed up at the Quarter Houses on a leash. The mighty Bozo, the Royal Leader of the Dawgs, on a leash? No, Mab."

I could hear Bozo grumbling. I screeched and hit F above high C. "Quit that, Bozo!" Bozo looked up me, the dark liquid eyes brimming with dog tears. "Big fat act, Bozo. You'd probably like to have my left thigh for dinner."

"You've hurt his feelings, Mab."

"I'd like to hurt his behind." With that, Bozo waddled to me and put his huge jaws on my ankle and began to tug me toward Charlie.

"What's he doing, Charlie? Help."

"You know he hates it when you yell at him. He just wants you to come over by me so you'll quit."

I moved toward Charlie and Bozo let go.

*   *   *   *

A truce was called after the Bulldog football season when Charlie acquiesced and put Bozo on a leash. As long as it wasn't football season, he reasoned, the mighty Bozo's image would remain untarnished. The Fanatics still clanged their cowbells anytime they saw Bozo and he obligingly left a part of himself in their yards. Now that Bozo looked under control, parents let their children pat his gigantic head. The drooling, bowlegged Bozo stood like a rock when a little one would squat down, lift up his dewlaps and shriek with laughter. He bore humiliation much better than I would have.

The day I took Bozo out by myself was the day the whole Bozo thing really blew out of proportion. He suddenly jerked the leash out of my hand and rocked across the street with me in shrill pursuit. Before my eyes, he pushed a wandering toddler to the curb as a car sped by so close that it grazed his butt. The child's hysterical mother appeared, snatched up her errant imp and declared Bozo a saint. Bozo toppled over and lay still. I thought he was dead. I kneeled beside him and stroked his ponderous head. I crooned that he was a hero and must not die because Charlie would be bereft and unfit to live with. Our marriage would be doomed.

It seemed that Saint Bozo was merely in temporary shock, and before I knew it he had risen and was slobbering all over my face with his huge slab of a tongue. I was so happy that he was alive that I hugged his neck and kissed his inky nose.

Charlie was smug and puffed with pride. He welcomed the Fanatics bearing meaty dog bones and treats for their hero. The mother of the runaway came by to thank Bozo and insisted that her precious child give Bozo a kiss. Bozo promptly bathed the child with his drool. The child squealed and whacked Bozo on the head. He never blinked.

Football season began again. The wives shopped for snacks, beer and onion dip. "It's for Saint Bozo, dear. He loves onion dip, you know." I moaned. Now the bouquet of Bozo's gastrointestinal expulsions would come home with him from every Quarter House, after every game.

*　　　*　　　*　　　*

I received a terrifying phone call just before half-time of the last game of the season. "Mabel, something's wrong with Charlie. I think he's had a stroke. I've called 911."

Bozo went crazy trying to get into the ambulance and I had to climb in with him to calm him. The orderlies were kind and let us stay with Charlie. My beloved died of a brain aneurysm before we reached the hospital.

My world crumbled, fractured and splintered. I dropped into depression soon after the numbing circus of well-wishers and food-bringers went back to their lives. I would have locked my shell tight around me, but Bozo had to do his dog thing. We walked deep into the woods surrounding our home every day, and I found myself confiding my grief to Bozo. I said awful things to God and about God, and life in general. Bozo just listened. I began calling him "Doctor B" and he'd come to me and grumble and slobber. He was my mourning blanket. I discarded my earplugs and gained comfort in his raspy snoring at night.

I had shut out the fact that the football season would begin again until the opening-game day when Bozo started acting nutso. He lumbered to the front door, then to me, to the front door, then to me, back and forth, back and forth, growling and grumbling fiercely. I thought he was deranged or was on the verge of a serious gastrointestinal blow out. I took a deep breath, shut my eyes, and let him out. He galumphed down the front steps with all the dignity an English Bulldog could muster. He pitched and rolled his way around to the Quarter Houses as cowbells rang and greetings were called. He returned to the house after the game and filled the air with eau de onion dip. When he looked at me, his whole lumpy, bowlegged body trembled and his big, dark eyes filled with tears.

My heart melted hot inside of me. "I know, Dr. B. You couldn't find Charlie. It's okay. He's in your heart just like he's in mine." I hugged his neck and we wept together.

Bozo continued to look for Charlie during every football game of the season. He received accolades, back scratching, and onion dip from each Fanatic at every Quarter House. The Board Letters ceased.

Bozo always started out hoping, and always came home exhausted and teary. It was his tribute to Charlie and I adored the big, sloppy, slobbery, odious dog for it.

Just to prove to the big clunker how much I loved him, I bought him a Bozoette. I figured it would keep him closer to home and out of trouble in the neighborhood. Am I a glutton for punishment, or what?

A Room without a View

By Ann Foskey

My old garage door was a part of the family. It was a loud, cantankerous grandpa living just outside the kitchen, sending us off with a shout each morning and tucking us in with a thump each night. Its old-fashioned windows were etched in dust, spider webs, and the impressions of a nine year-old's fingerprints. It was made from wood–painted pine boards–perhaps from one of the last lumberyards in nearby Woodstock.

Held together by hinges and screws, this grumpy gatekeeper was constantly exfoliating. Pieces and parts would mysteriously appear in my path—a little nut here, a little bolt there. "Where did this lug come from?" I wondered. The lawn-mower? The weed whacker? A bike? I ignored the voice in my head telling me to investigate. "Oh well," I thought, "into the junk drawer it goes."

The door's process of letting go went on for months, over a period of three years. One day it lost its last screw and refused to close. It simply stopped, locked in place. Its arthritic joints could no longer make the journey over the curved track. Panes were lifted from their courses, threatening to pop from the frames and crash to the floor. We worked for hours to resuscitate it, but it was beyond repair.

A handyman friend came over to help remove the door from the house. With slow, steady steps the men carried the long boards to the back of the house, care-fully leaning them against a crumbling wall where it would lie in repose.

Life goes on. I had to leave to take my son to a birthday party. When I returned, my husband had ordered a new garage door. My heart sank when I saw it. It was thoroughly modern. The door was made of some space-age polymer–but well insulated. The windows were high up, too high to see in or out–but safe. Safe and insulated—hallmarks of the 21st century.

Now, when I take my morning walks through my quietly-aging neighbor-hood, I look with fondness upon the original garage doors that still stand. They are familiar to me, companionable, like old timers relaxing on the porch, holding up the houses. I wish I had paid just a little more attention to those loose screws.

Tree Bark and Tadpoles

By Kathleen Craft Boehmig

A bridge of salty freckles
Across a sweaty nose;
Ten dirty little fingernails,
More dirt between his toes.

Tree bark in the bedsheets,
Tadpoles in the tub;
There's no doubt about it,
It's a stinky boy I love!

He loves gross bugs and slimy things,
Computers and cartoons;
Lightnin' bugs and fishing,
Rock collecting and raccoons.

He writes adventure stories
And draws pictures with great flair.
He screams and tries to run
When we, unheeding, brush his hair.

Tree bark in the bedsheets,
Tadpoles in the tub;
There's no doubt about it,
It's a stinky boy I love!

He loves to make up silly songs
Like "Hound dogs on the moon"
Which he will gladly sing for us—
We love to hear him croon.

At end of day, he takes a bath
And slips between the sheets;
Makes praying hands and says his prayers
And in a voice so sweet

He says, "I love you, Mama"
Like an angel from above.
I wouldn't trade the tree-bark,
Or the tadpoles in the tub.

There just is no denying
It's a precious boy I love!

Pantoum of Truth

By Paul A. Bussard

Truth is a fractal. It tiles the universe.
Truth will transcend Time.
Order within Chaos, Chaos within Order,
Truth is most interesting at its edges.

Truth will transcend Time.
Infinitely consistent, nowhere the same,
Truth is most interesting at its edges.
We can never know Truth—only little truths.

Infinitely consistent, nowhere the same,
Truth and Comfort—Yin and Yang,
We can never know Truth—only little truths.
Comfort is our aperture on Truth.

Truth and Comfort—Yin and Yang,
Truth is naked; we clothe it for our own comfort.
Comfort is our aperture on Truth.
There is only one Truth, but infinite apertures.

Truth is naked; we clothe it for our own comfort.
Truth is a Möbius strip; there is always a twist.
There is only one Truth, but infinite apertures.
The other side of Truth is also true.

Truth is a Möbius strip; there is always a twist.
Order within Chaos, Chaos within Order,
The other side of Truth is also true.
Truth is a fractal. It tiles the universe.

Any Questions, Master Gardeners?

By John Sheffield

Many years ago, my master gardener wife and I took our youngest son, Nick, for riding lessons. At the end of the lesson, the young riders were grouped around their intimidating instructor.

"Any questions?" she barked at the students perched on their steeds, whacking her riding crop on her boot.

Nick, age four, tentatively raised his hand.

"Yes, Nicholas."

"What was the name of the first lion killed?" Nicholas asked.

"What kind of a stupid question is that? Obviously, I meant questions about riding and horses."

"But you said, 'Any questions?'"

When we left the riding stables, we found out what Nick was asking. He had heard the story of Androcles and the Lion, was confused, and worried about the lion.

He was right, though. She had said, "Any questions?" How often do we hear this said or implied, and what are the consequences?

If you are a master gardener volunteering at the Help Desk in the North Fulton Extension Office, operated by the University of Georgia, you should be prepared to answer "any questions."

Ring! Ring! The master gardener picked up the phone.

"I'm with the Atlanta Zoo," the man on the line said. "We have a problem with the monkeys." Hearing no response, he continued, "They have diarrhea."

"I'll put you on the speaker phone so that my colleague can hear your question. What is it, exactly?"

"When the monkeys walk across their compound, they drag their hands on the ground and keep getting re-infected."

"I see. What gardening information would you like from us?"

"How can we sterilize the ground?"

The two gardeners in the Extension Office each made a face. "Give us your phone number and someone will call you back." The last resort for difficult questions, as always, was the knowledgeable and long-suffering County Extension Agent.

The Smith Plantation House is a favorite stop for school groups and hosts a summer camp for younger students. The grounds contain a true bog that is sustained by seepage from springs. One day, a master gardener was planting Louisiana irises and pitcher plants, when her waders sank so far into the wet ground that she could not move. Thank heavens the young children can't see me, she thought, imagining their questions as she extricated herself using a shovel.

"What are you doing?" "Are you stuck?" "Why are you stuck?" "If I help you, will I get stuck, too?" "My dad got stuck once."

She thought of an answer to save for a future occasion, "I'm making a hole for this iris," she would say.

Some years ago, a plumber was fixing pipes under the Summerour Farm House at Autrey Mill. Soon after he had started work, he rushed into the director's office. "Some idiot is throwing clods of dirt at me," he said angrily, "You've got to tell them to stop!"

"That's terrible," she said. "Let me see what I can do."

The director followed him back to the work place, staying for a while but only she and the plumber were present, and she returned to her office.

Some time later, the plumber stormed back in. "I've had enough of it," he said. "Somebody's still throwing dirt at me." He left.

The director searched again, but she was alone with the clods. Who do you call about ghosts?

A master gardener was showing the Butterfly Garden, one of five theme gardens at Bulloch Hall, to a visiting group. "This bush is a favorite of our butterflies," she said.

As she pointed at a flower, a butterfly circled and landed on it.

"How did you do that?" a visitor asked.

"Training," she replied with a smile.

At High Meadows School in Roswell, the Junior Master Gardeners—seven-to-nine years old—have a program called, "Plant a Row for the Hungry." By early June of 2006, they had already given forty-five pounds of squash to the Food Bank.

In answer to your question, "Will there be more?" The answer is yes—tomatoes, peppers, and sweet potatoes are on their way.

At the Williams-Payne House, the site of the original springs for which Sandy Springs is named, one of the activities is recreating a typical vegetable garden of the 1860's, planting only seeds. An occasional difficulty for the master gardeners is working out whether what emerges from the ground is what they planted, because some of the traditional crops, such as crowder peas, are not common today. Early on, an unknown plant appeared that rapidly grew to tower over the Milk House—a true Jack-in-the Beanstalk affair. They called experts at the University of Georgia. Finding out that it was not a vegetable, they cut it down before it reached high enough for the giant to descend.

Back at the Extension Office, the questions are still coming in.
Ring! Ring! "How can we help you?"
"I've had this plant in my garage for three days and I can't plant it. What should I do?"
"Why can't you plant it?"
"It's been foggy and cloudy."
"And?"
"It says on the label, 'Plant in full sun.'"

Sometimes, the caller into the Extension Office will present a question in a peculiar way. "My English Ivy is dying."
The two gardeners manning the phone gaped. "How did you manage that?" they asked, laughing.
"I'm serious."
"Oh, you are? You know many people want to get rid of that stuff? Where do you live? Somebody should come and find out your secret to success."

Ring! Ring! "How can I help you?"
"I landscaped this new subdivision and put in a row of trees along the median of the road...they all look like they're dying. I'm standing by them right now. What can I do?"
"Pull back the mulch and tell me what you see."
"There's some orange cord around the trunk."
"Scrape some more and tell me what you see."
"It looks like burlap bag."
"So you didn't cut back the bags and remove the cords when you put the trees in. Now the roots can't grow out and the cord is strangling the trunk. What kind of trees are they?"
"Bradford pears."
"Well. I have good new and bad news."
"What's the bad news?"

"The trees have to go."

"And the good news?"

"They're Bradford pears."

"I'm not sure whether you're the right people," the caller said hesitantly, "but we have a problem with a sofa."

"A sofa?"

"It smells a bit and needs cleaning."

"Why?"

"Well you see, our uncle died, and we didn't discover the body for a few days. He was on the sofa. Now we want to clean it…." A long silence followed. "It's a good sofa."

Even the County Extension Agent could not have helped with that one.

This is the mission statement of the Georgia Master Gardeners Association:

"To stimulate the love for and increase the knowledge of gardening, and to voluntarily and enthusiastically share this knowledge with others."

Given what happens, it looks as if it would be a good idea to add, "Be prepared to answer questions on anything."

The master gardeners are residents of the local community who have an active interest in gardening and in sharing their knowledge with others. They must satisfactorily complete an extensive horticultural training program to become qualified. In addition to providing advice at the Extension Office, they are involved in major activities at seven sites.	1845 Archibald Smith Plantation House in Roswell. Autrey Mill Nature Preserve in Alpharetta. Big Trees Forest Preserve in Sandy Springs. Bulloch Hall in Roswell. Habitat for Humanity houses in North Fulton. Projects at school grounds. 1869 Williams-Payne House in Sandy Springs.

Crossing the Chattahoochee

By Rob Elliott

The artillery gathered along our side of the Chattahoochee is what's left of the Chicago Board of Trade Battery, consisting of four guns dug into the soft clay along the bluffs of the river. Last night we worked long hours to clear the trees and brush to make room for the guns and were kindly praised by the artillerymen who thanked us by preparing a breakfast this morning of blackberries and milk. We sat in small circles around our campfires and talked of homes, farms, and sweethearts while Eli Lane, who's in my mess, said the war is just as good as over now. When I looked down at my light blue trousers, ripped and muddied and too big to fit me anymore, I wished he was right.

The forest along the bank of the Chattahoochee River is thick. Huge oaks and poplars reaching out from the cracks of rocky slopes and, of course, the pine trees squeezed in so close together they can't grow but half-sized—their little needles dwarfed from lack of sunlight. Between it all and tangling the ground, the brush makes it near impossible to see anything between the trees and perhaps if a rebel, with his butternut hued uniform, is moving around in there, I might not ever see him.

What glory, I think. How lucky I am to be a part of the first assault on Roswell, the first steps of many before the glorious taking of Atlanta. I am to be counted among the soldiers who will open the back gate of the city for General Sherman. What a glorious honor for such an ordinary man in such an unordinary time.

The guns and artillerymen are working now in the morning fog, the thunder of each shot echoing off the river's surface and bouncing back at us from every direction. They are ripping the earth apart. The guns are quite a thing to hear, let me tell you. The pounding and the shaking of the earth. I swear God is going to descend right then and there and say: "Stop all this racket here." The strange thing is that, through the explosions and deafening thunder, I can still hear the faint croaking of a frog near the river shore, lost in the haze which has settled upon the land, just going about his business as if this noise, marking this a day of reckoning for us all, don't bother him none at all.

Our battalion, consisting of the 72nd and the 17th Indiana, stands in battle line on the slope of a hill that descends down to the Chattahoochee. On the opposite side of the river, situated on a much higher rise in the land are several regiments of rebel militia guarding what is left of this hot and sticky land. *This is it,* I think. *This is what soldiering is all about…an honest fight.* Only the river stands between us.

Colonel Miller rides swiftly to the front on a fine gray horse and positions himself between us and the boys from the 17th Indiana. While an aide secures the reigns, the colonel swings his feet from the stirrups and dismounts. It is customary for the officers of our regiment to give a few words of encouragement before we engage the enemy, and today is no different. He mentions the fact that the rebels on the other side of the river are already running away in fright, then he calls out several companies from both regiments as skirmishers. My company, company D, is one of them.

Captain Thompson, a gentleman and our beloved leader, looks surprised that our company is selected for such an honor, then hollers an unfamiliar command. "FIRST PLATOON…AS SKIRMISHERS."

The boys in our company are confused at what this command means and we all jostle between one another, our accoutrements, pans, and tin cups clinking together in confusion. We hear the captain's voice through our bewildered mumbles. "ON THE LEFT FILE…TAKE INTERVALS…MARCH!"

It has long been my habit, when perplexed by the orders of Captain Thompson, to simply follow the man in front of me. When I see that this method does not work, I then look around at what the man beside me is doing. By the time I figure things out, I realize that we are forming a long skirmish line, all of us spread out and positioned at zigzagging intervals.

The bugles sound giving us the order to move the skirmish line forward and down the sloping hill to the river. A skirmish line is much different than a line of battle, in that the men are spread out instead of marching shoulder-to-shoulder. I now realize how precarious a spot I am in, by not being protected by a man in front of me. There is nothing to shield me, save for the trees and my love for God.

Thorn bushes make for a thousand obstacles as we ease down the slope, such that when a man's trousers or brogans get snagged upon a vine, he must pause a moment to unravel himself. Because this happens all across the line, the advance is slow and cautious as if we are tramping through a den of angry water-moccasins. One twisted vine is mean enough to leap up from Eli's foot as he passes by and strikes my knee. It impales its fangs all the way through the thin flesh of my kneecap and draws a right amount of blood. I holler out in pain and Eli, who marches in a crouch in front of me, is careful for now on to gently move the vines away with the butt of his rifle and not let them backlash me when he passes through.

When we reach the bottom of the hill at the bank of the river, I witness a scene that reminds me much of the spectacle that took place during the barn raising we did for my cousins back four summers past. That day, the young men from our settlement, many of whom now march in the skirmish line, gathered for the barn raising. We had just got the foundation dug when the sky grew dark and the rain began. It came down in buckets and wet us all, soaked us to the very pulp. Try as we might, we couldn't grab hold of a log without it slipping from our hands and splashing up a great deal of mud when it plopped to the ground. And that mud went everywhere…on our shirts, pants, and specially our faces. Where the foundation was dug, the mud got so deep it swallowed our feet when we stepped in it. Before too long, we lost our shoes in the depths of the mud and took up the soft ground between our toes.

Of course, not being able to raise the barn troubled us. But just when we couldn't get any angrier in our struggle to sit those logs up, we gave into laughing. Each took up handfuls of the sloppy mud and slung it at one another until we were just covered in the stuff. We soon found ourselves engaged in a mud battle of sorts, standing in two opposing lines and throwing it just as fast as we could scoop it up…

Without a single warning comes a noise like nothing I've ever heard. *Zzzippp, zzzippp, thwack.* Directly over our heads, the air splits apart. Something like a winged bug hurries by, and flutters on behind us through the woods until it finally hits a tree. *Zzzippp, zzzippp, thwack.* This is not a crowd of boys slinging mud at one another, or even the things old veterans tell about in their stories. These are real bullets. We are being shot at.

This is when I slip at last and fall into the rift of madness. The tragedy I thought would never come to pass, because life surely ain't that cruel, suddenly becomes real. Some of the boys might pretend it's nothing but a story, something you might hear around a late night jug of the O Be Joyful. Others have the knack to just shrug it off. But for me, it is real all right. Bright as day and just as clear. The world *does* work that way, just the way I always feared it would be, even if I prayed to God. I find the reason for my fear and why I'm afraid of this war so very much. Those moments of terror I've felt in the past, have always been just short little visits to this real place of madness. I've always been let out and released from it before. But when I see Eli Lane, my friend and pard, get shot in the jaw right there on the bank of the Chattahoochee it's enough to bury me in that hole of madness for good.

A soldier in battle, more often than not, will shoot at the enemy who is shooting directly at him. That is the way men fight. On this particular day, however, the rebels are hidden on the far side of a river, buried deep in the foliage and brush. Because we cannot see our enemy, we fire our rifles, one shot after another, into the blind. Our Spencer rifles can be loaded from the rear and have a faster rate of fire than the more common muzzle-loading rifles, such as the Springfield and the Enfield. We always considered ourselves as having an advantage in weaponry with these fast loading rifles, but now, when we cannot see the enemy, our fears are multiplied.

"Captain Thompson!" A man further down the skirmish line wails over the blasts of rifles. "Come quickly, Eli is hit!"

I hear a whisper near my ear, a feller saying ever so quietly: "Somebody shut that boy up."

"DOCTOR ABRAHAM! SURGEON! QUICKLY…"

"Hush damn you."

I can now hear Eli moaning softly in the mud and fog. A dog barks from the top of the slope, getting nearer as it races down toward the water and the den of battle. It is Dixie, our company dog and mascot. We give her that name to honor the fact that we found her in this land of the South, living off scraps of salt pork offered to her by the boys of our company. Her loyalties obviously lie with the Union by the way she took to the boys in blue and followed us down the dusty roads all the way here to Roswell. Before Dixie can reach our injured pard, a rebel bullet finds its mark. It enters Eli's forehead at such an angle that it forces his neck backwards. His spine makes a disturbing noise when it snaps.

His body slides in the soft clay, down the slope where the water swallows him. Eli is carried gently down stream, as if rocked in a cradle or the in the arms of his dear old momma.

"You don't mean to say that we are expected to wade across that river?" says a nearby voice. Before I realize the consequences of such a suicidal march, the bugles sound for advance, and we are up and moving into the cold water of the Chattahoochee. When I am knee deep, I take a glace back at the bank where Dixie stands in mud barking at us in encouragement.

Now let me tell you, trying to walk across the bottom of a river, fully clothed and strapped to a pair of old brogans is not a task easily accomplished. There are rocks at the bottom of a river, slimy rocks that will slip your feet from underneath you. There are currents down there too that will pull you downriver if you let them get the better of you. Not to mention the bullets buzzing over the surface of the water, right at level with your eyes, right where you can actually see the hot lead and feel the stinging in your ears.

Back on the Union side of the river, I can hear a voice shouting over the pops of our rifles. "Bully boys!" says the voice that might be the colonel. "Whisky in the morning!"

A gurgling war cry erupts from the water, a soggy shout that that makes us want to run forward in a pulse of excitement. Because we wade neck deep in the river now, it is impossible to match the exhilaration of our shouts by running under water. In fact, it is near impossible to move forward at all. We are stuck quick in the river. It is a turkey shoot, with our very heads being the exposed targets as we shiver with cold and fear. It is all we can do to move forward, ever so slowly, ever so carefully.

During the charge, our heads bob in the river and I gasp for quick breaths taking in more water than air. One man disappears into the river and I don't know if he has lost his balance or if he has been mortally wounded. More men are now floating down the river upon their backs and upon their stomachs, already bloating in the hot July sun. Another man from the 17th raises his soggy rifle from the river. "Damn you," he shouts. "Damn all of you." He makes as if to discharge his weapon, to show the rebels we mean business.

Imagine our surprise when we see the puff of smoke and hear the crack of his river-soaked rifle. The rear loading Spencer uses a metallic cartridge that, we quickly find out, is water-proof. Upon seeing the head of this man from the 17th Indiana emerge from beneath the water with his rifle brought to sights, then fire off an expert shot as if to defy the very laws of the natural world, we all realize that fate has indeed, in some small way, smiled upon us this day.

I move faster through the river now, raising my rifle, firing off a shot, then ducking back down into the water and safety. Rebel bullets splash all around me, making a soft *plunk* as they dive into the depths where the lead quickly cools to hard and deadly shapes. Some bullets skip off the surface of the water, like stones in a child's game. Others bury themselves into flesh and bone.

With a shout, greater than before, I arrive on the other side. All down the skirmish line, soggy men in blue drag themselves out of the river, their wool uniforms heavy and dripping with water. Although it appears a sorry sight to me, the image of hundreds of soldiers emerging from the river still firing shots from their water-logged rifles, frightens the few remaining rebels. To them, we are surely the very creatures of hell, rising from the depths. Up against such a supernatural enemy, the only choice is but to flee. As I steal a glace behind me, I can see the remainder of our battalion crossing the Chattahoochee in similar fashion, with the same gazes of amazement impressed upon their faces.

I might not ever understand the ways of war, why it takes us on a path full of twists and turns through many a dense forest and blinding storm. Suppose war exists to teach us something. What, then, would the lesson be? We must learn to accept the death of our brothers; we must learn to accept the death of ourselves. Or maybe a soldier's life is just a step in the process God uses to form the soul into what He wants it to be, like a potter might shape a lump of clay into the form of a bowl and place it in the kiln to harden. Sometimes the heat in this kiln gets too hot and burns a small dark spot in the clay. This is when war hurts us and leaves an ugly scar.

On the other side of the river, the scars are many. Our trousers, blouses, and haversacks are soaked through and through, leaving our corn meal and crackers moldy and our bellies cold and hungry. After the last of the rebels have been driven off, some of the boys thought to string up fishing poles fashioned from thread and old knotty branches. They had naught to use for bait except some broken up hardtack which did not attract the attention of the fish none too well. There is not much else we can do for grub, seeing as how the wagons cannot cross the river here. Captain Thompson says that it will be safe enough for the wagons to cross at the ferry in two days, when this side of the river is clear of rebels.

As the sun begins to set I wander off from camp, hungry and tired, feeling lost in this strange forest. I think of Eli who was swept off down the river before witnessing the great miracle of today. Somehow, amidst the loneliness, I muster the energy to do something about our pitiful state. I take my Spencer rifle, holler for Dixie, our company hound, and sneak out into the woods to scare up a deer. Dixie is a first rate hunting dog and is suitable for just about any game. She's very loyal and, if she has a mind to, can kill a deer all by herself. Which is a good thing, because right now I don't believe I could kill one myself.

The woods surrounding this town of Roswell are thick and full of game, so it's not long before I spot a buck and, with a shaking finger, fire off a shot. The bullet passes through the buck's right thigh and wounds him only slightly. Just like we've taught her, Dixie sets to barking her head off and chases the buck all the way to the bank of the Chattahoochee. There she goes through the trees and down the hill. The wool of my uniform is still wet and heavy and my brogans feel like stones tied to my feet. When I finally catch up to her, Dixie has the buck cornered at the edge of the river where an old tree has fallen and blocks access to the water. Dixie has her teeth dug into the deer's throat. She growls and bites at the same time, tearing a flap of hide from his neck.

Both animals roll on the ground, stirring up the dead leaves around them, and making it difficult for me to tell dog from buck. Certainly, I don't want to take the chance of shooting Dixie on accident, so I walk around to the side of them, looking for a clear shot. Mostly I think on what a good supper I'm going to bring back to the boys, as I watch the buck rear and flop about most frantically. I'm squeezing the trigger, when the buck suddenly gives one good kick to Dixie's underside, which makes her wail out in pain. The kick is powerful and knocks the dog loose from the buck's throat. Dixie howls through the air, lifting a distance of some ten or twenty yards.

I should shoot the deer now. That would be the end of it. But that is not what happens. In these few moments, after Dixie has been kicked away, I sit crouched on one knee and simply watch in awe. The buck sneezes, blows air out his snout, and bends down so his sharp antlers aim right for my head. Believing I am about to be impaled on the horns of a deer, I shut tight my eyes, bracing for its charge by holding forth my rifle in the *guard against cavalry* position. Captain Thompson taught us this stance, a basic part of the manual-of-arms drill, but I never thought I'd be using it in a situation like this.

The buck's hooves trample the leaves on the ground as he runs at me. I don't see any of this, for my eyes are closed. There's a moment of panic, and I reach down into my trousers pocket to where a knife is hidden beneath some broken pieces of soggy cracker. My *guard against cavalry* is a useless maneuver. Without a bayonet attached to the Spencer rifle, I might as well be holding a tree branch or other such useless thing.

I open my eyes and witness a true miracle. The buck charges me at full stride, a strip of his flesh whipping against his neck from where Dixie had chewed him raw. He is upon me, and suddenly he stops. His legs wobble in terror, but somehow the buck finds the strength to slowly raise its front hooves and, with awkward and jerky movements, he places both of his skinny legs upon my shoulders. The poor beast is so scared of Dixie and her snapping jaws he has run to me for safety. As if I am his mother, the buck nuzzles his head up to the side of my neck, and lays his face on my cheek. He blows air from his nose, which tickles warmly in my ear. I don't know if deer are able to do such a thing, but I also hear him whine.

Dixie is now up from the ground, and staggering towards the deer. Her bark is not as loud, due to having her wind knocked out, but she comes barking up to the wounded deer all the same. She aims to finish him off. But before she can, I set my rifle to the ground and take out my pocket knife from underneath the crackers. While I hold the top of the buck's head steady, and while he rubs his cold nose across my face, I slit the poor thing's throat.

Before I bring the meat back to camp, with the deer's blood still wet on my arm, I sit down under an old sycamore tree on the bank of the Chattahoochee and weep.

Free

By Terry Segal

This man I've never met lies in a wooden box before me. A chorus of angels sings hymns from on high, and everything is white. Everything but the black stories that bog my mind and create a cognitive dissonance as I sit on sharp pickets between this world and that.

Two years of tales from the daughter of Darkness turn my fertile, pulsing heart to stone; a stone colder than the one that will mark his grave in the ice storms of Georgia's winters. No tears are mine as I sit in a sea of salt from the flooding waters around me.

I send a light of shining armor to engulf her as she moves to speak through her instrument. It wails the pain of the past and trills the flight of the butterfly wings in his garden. The bow, laid heavy on the strings, is like his now cold body that never should have touched hers, his wounds bleeding on to her until she didn't know who bled.

I stare through tar-colored glasses at the face in the photo resembling hers. The hand of the grieving widow on my shoulder turns me around. "He was such a wonderful man," she says. All I can see is the shell of a woman who had to know.

Where is my misplaced heart? It holds the string of words I'm supposed to give her for comfort. She gets none from me. She knows that her family will never again be forced to have Thanksgiving dinner with the rapist. No more separation from the grandkids she pretended was from distance, rather than restraining orders to protect them. An empty chair in the kiddie porn chat room waits for some other tortured wretch to inhabit.

I pay no respects. I'm here solely for her—for her soul. It is the soul of an enchanting goddess in a white gown who carries a black cloak she was told she could never put down.

Outside again, when she numbly dons it, I will sweep the hood from her face, releasing her raven locks, and implore the winds to blow it from her corporeal being, freeing her from it forevermore. "Torch the dank and dusky cloak," I will scream, "and send up the ash as burnt offerings to the maker of those scorched memories; a twisted, haunted spirit whom I know you also loved. Say goodbye now and free yourself," I will tell her. "Rise from the darkened, spiraling vortex to twirl like a cherry blossom, loosed from the spiny branch that held you fast. Twirl, twirl, twirl, sweet goddess. Twirl until you are free."

A Southern California Brat Migrates To Georgia

By Judy Parker-Matz

—Running Away from the Southern California Lifestyle—

Eleven years ago, I ran away from home, home being Diamond Bar, California, a bedroom community and suburb of Los Angeles located twenty-five miles southeast from the city center. A bedroom community, as described by me, is a town without industry. It's a compilation of, mostly, single-family dwellings where the population is living the middle-class, American dream.

To this particular point in time, I'd always been a Californian…born and raised in the Southland, the land of "fruits and nuts," where Hollywood collides with the jet set. It's true that roughly a quarter of the population of the entire USA lives there, so one can find ethnic and socio-economic diversity anywhere within the state. Yes, the mega rich often reside adjacent to the very poor and anyone can certainly create or conceive any reality or lifestyle they wish to pursue. But, overall, the bulk of the Southern California population is really no different than any other American. They're working as hard and have the same concerns and issues as anyone else living in the United States. They're just crammed into the Los Angeles basin like sardines in a can! And they scurry about like rats in a maze. Over the years as the population exploded so did the concrete and asphalt infrastructure to support it. Amidst this explosion, the sense of community has greatly diminished as has the human connection to the natural world.

It was a lifestyle I came to abhor and a distant departure from the environment in which I had been reared. California in the 1950s still had wide-open spaces and *Leave It to Beaver*-type neighborhoods. I grew up in one. I lived on a cul-de-sac where there were lots of kids my age and we played outdoors on summer evenings until it got too dark to see and our parents forced us inside. We built forts. We climbed trees. We swam in the community swimming pool. We walked everywhere and visited the corner store for penny candy. The bread man and milkman still delivered door-to-door and all the neighbors knew each other. It was wonderful to be a child in Southern California in the 1950s.

—California Distinctions and/or Dreams Turned Into Nightmares?—

Alas, there are a few things that do set Southern California apart from the rest of the country. One of them is the weather, which, I think, was the premiere drawing card for the hordes that migrated there after World War II. I've often joked with my new southern friends that Southern California doesn't DO weather, and with an average yearly rainfall of only eleven inches, it doesn't!

Nobody in California watches the Weather Channel, whereas, in Georgia, it can be a gripping television drama. I've been known to spend hours glued to the set watching the latest updates to the Doppler radar tracking that funnel cloud that could be headed my way. For the same reason, Californians don't have houses with basements. Tornadoes, or any kind of electrical storms, are an extreme exception.

But, I hear you saying, California does have earthquakes, which certainly sets it apart from anywhere else in the country and seems to strike terror in all Americans who've never experienced one. I must admit, they are unsettling. It's an insecure and disorienting feeling to have the earth move underneath your feet. But, frankly, after experiencing numerous earthquakes during my tenure in California, I find them less terrifying than huddling in the basement waiting for the tornado to pass...with the Civil Defense sirens blaring, the wind howling, and the Weather Channel announcing that the funnel cloud is headed directly for my house.

But don't misunderstand me; I much prefer the drama of the southern spring-time storms to the non-weather of California. Certainly, in California, the seasons change but they don't do it with the flair or beauty that I've experienced in the South. The Georgia springtime is a sight to behold as the trees unfurl new leaves in all shades of green, the dogwoods bloom, the pines produce enough pollen to create yellow rain that falls on everything, and the flowers explode with vibrant colors. Springtime in Georgia is gorgeous!

One of the other Southern California distinctions that Golden Stators always mention is that you can get to the mountains, the ocean, and the desert within an hour or two from anywhere within the Los Angeles basin. Nowhere in the country can you snow ski in the morning and watch the sunset over the ocean in the evening. That's assuming you can fight your way across the congested interstate highways to get from one place to the other.

I left behind the pristine beaches where I spent all my childhood and adolescent vacations because, as an adult, it was such an ordeal to get there, park, and find a spot large enough to lay down a towel amidst the thousands of others (and I do mean THOUSANDS) who were there enjoying the sun and surf.

—Creating the New Life...—

So, yes, I'm a disgruntled California brat who ran away from home to Georgia so many years ago. In 1995, I was so totally disenchanted with the urban sprawl, being isolated in my neighborhood, the commute to and from a corporate job, the horrendous air pollution and the gang violence that sporadically affected my life…I was ready to recreate my life elsewhere.

On the other side of the country, Atlanta was preparing to host the 1996 Olympic games and its economy was beginning to boom. The job market was bustling, which provided me with numerous opportunities for career growth, the weather was warm enough to accommodate my thin blood, and housing was affordable!

I fell in love with Georgia at first sight. Flying over Atlanta gave me my first glimpse of a sea of green…TREES. Trees, trees and more trees…the pines, oaks, dogwoods, and the fast-growing sweet gums, not to mention the ever-creeping Japanese kudzu (whose idea was that, anyway?). Once on the ground, safely ensconced in my rental car and driving north up the infamous Georgia 400 to Alpharetta, I got to experience the blue, blue sky combined with the white puffy clouds and the green trees that created a picture I'd only seen before in magazines like the National Geographic. What a departure from the perpetual gray of the Southern California smog.

Besides the trees and the blue sky, which stood in total contrast to the arid desert next to the ocean where I grew up, my first impressions also included a slower pace of life than I was used to living. I recall standing in line at Kroger and becoming more and more impatient as the clerk and customers exchanged pleasantries in thick, southern drawls…no hurries, no worries.

"How are the kids doin' in school?"

"Who won the baseball game yesterday?"

Here was a sense of community that existed in this northern Atlanta suburb that had long since disappeared in California where hurry, hurry, scurry, scurry was the norm. I had to remind myself that I had no appointments, no reason to be in a rush; just take the time to watch and enjoy the human interaction taking place in front of me. I actually had time to breathe the fresh air and let the stress of Southern California ebb away.

Yes, Georgia felt like home. It felt like the California where I'd grown up before it got overly populated and polluted. In 1995, Alpharetta was still Georgia horse country (parts of that heritage still exist west of the Georgia 400 in 2006) and was largely undeveloped. Subdivisions and shopping centers were just beginning to pop up here and there amongst the trees. People waved at you (and still do) as you drove down suburban streets. No matter that they didn't know you from Adam's cat, they were just naturally friendly.

And courtesy on the roadways? Unbelievable and nonexistent in the Southern California I left behind where road rage was…all the rage! These southern folks actually stopped to let you turn into traffic from a side street instead of hitting the gas pedal to make certain you couldn't arrive at your destination one car length or ten seconds ahead of them.

Vacant land and woods existed where kids could disappear and play. The corner store still existed, too, as did the family-run restaurants on town squares. Not only that, I came to know all my neighbors…by face and name! We actually have neighborhood ice cream socials and holiday parties, not to mention providing tremendous support and compassion in times of need.

—The Signatures of the South—

Today, I live on a small, man-made lake in Cumming, Georgia, where I can maintain a semblance of the illusion that I'm still living the suburban-country lifestyle. After only four years living in this lovely setting, urban sprawl is beginning to creep into my world once more. All around me, trees are disappearing and structures are replacing them. Highways are choked with automobiles and what used to be quaint country roads are now gridlocked thoroughfares.

Yet, many aspects of the Southern, suburban-country life do still exist. You don't have to go far to find a glass of sweet tea, which is something this Southern California lady had never experienced prior to moving here and sorely misses whenever she visits northern or western states. There are rules for making good sweet tea. Adding sugar to cold iced tea after it's been brewed, as you do anywhere else in the country, tastes "different" as any good ole' Southern boy or girl will tell you. For true, Southern, sweet tea, the sugar has to be added while the tea is hot!

Another hallmark and certainly well represented in the northern Atlanta suburbs is the famed Waffle House restaurant. It's a highly successful restaurant chain located on just about every major intersection of any suburb…it's almost a requirement that there be a church (any denomination you prefer) right across the street. They're usually small, sparse, stand-alone buildings with yellow and black signage that blare its name: WAFFLE HOUSE. They cater to EVERY-BODY and they're open twenty-four hours a day, 365 days a year.

The help is "down home" Southern and the food is greasy, but it's also consistent, just like the McDonald's hamburger. You know what you're gonna get: (colon instead of ellipsis) hash browns, diced, smothered and peppered (which means they're cooked with onions, tomatoes, and jalapenos…yum, just the way I like them); the order screamed by the waitress to the cook who's standing two feet away.

The Southern drawl is thick, the food is inexpensive, and you can hobnob with many a true redneck who drives a Dodge Ram truck and has a Confederate flag waving in the breeze from a specially mounted antenna on the hood. My goodness, don't forget the NRA sticker glued to the back window or the country music booming from the radio as they speed by. These folks are the salt of the earth; good, hardworking people, with warm hearts and strong views on almost any subject and, most certainly, are descendents of folks from the Civil War era.

This is a bewilderment to the transplanted westerner; the Southerner's loyalty to the Confederacy. Initially I thought the attitudes were archaic and the flying of the Confederate flag quaint. The natives have long since given me a clear understanding of the way of life that was destroyed during the Civil War. Many of the white folks lost everything they'd worked for generations to build regardless of their attitudes or disposition toward slavery. The Yankee carpetbaggers who raped the South after that ill-fated conflict are still thought of with utter contempt and distain. It's taken over one hundred years for the South to rebuild and fully recover but, obviously, they have done so with a flourish. Atlanta is the hub and is rapidly becoming the Los Angeles of the South (with all its disturbing attributes).

However, native Georgians continue to respect their heritage by flying the flag from their porches or trucks and visiting the Stone Mountain laser show on hot, humid summer evenings. There they honor their country-music stars with lights blazing against the largest bas-relief granite carving in the country (if not the world) depicting their heroes, the three Confederates who led them in defeat. Elvis sings "Dixie" and the show closes with his version of the "Battle Hymn of the Republic." Baseball caps fly into the air and the whoops and hollers from the crowd are astounding. The Confederacy lives on and it's a unique historical perspective that bonds the people to the Southern way of life.

—It's About the Plant and Wildlife—

I've become a gardener since moving to Georgia. One must understand that land is a premium in Southern California. Your typical, middle-class home is normally located on a very small plot. Hence, there's not a tremendous amount of space where one can grow trees, flowers, or vegetables. And life's pace and the arid climate don't make gardening an attractive hobby either. I've found that digging in the Georgia clay is better than psychotherapy and watching the flowers bloom and growing a small portion my own food fulfilling.

But, far and away, for me, the most thrilling aspect of living in Georgia has been experiencing the local wildlife, which is nearly non-existent in Southern California's concrete jungle. From the deck of my home, I've spent many a peaceful hour watching the birds, the waterfowl, the rodents, and amphibious creatures.

Squirrels scamper and play in the trees. They chatter and swish their tails at my cats in sincere indignation for invading their territory. And, oh, yes, they also raid my bird feeders regularly.

The birds that come to feed are numerous (the cardinal, wren, chickadee, tit-mouse to name but a few) and I've learned their migratory patterns and welcome those who are just passing through along with those who stay year-round. I've had a majestic osprey grace us with his presence. Hawks land in my trees and sur-vey their territory. Egrets and herons eat the koi from the neighbors' ponds and the kingfisher trolls the lake daily for fish. Hummingbirds play and fight over their feeders and provide constant entertainment as they cheep and chase one another.

Did you ever notice that the blue jays are the policemen of the forest? They look like they're wearing uniforms with a black, pointed cap and distinctive blue and black body markings. They squawk and warn all the woodland creatures when a hawk is nearby and then, the entire surroundings become eerily quiet until the predator has flown away.

My yellow tabby cat, Tramp, who is the king of his own jungle, one day caught an Eastern bluebird, and the blue jays and the red-headed woodpeckers attempted to come to its rescue. I happened onto the scene to find my mighty hunter, bluebird in his mouth, cowering as he was assaulted by these large birds swooping down and pecking at his head. Sadly, the bluebird died but, for me, it was a wildlife lesson I'll never forget. They attempt to protect their own. The for-est has a set of rules I don't quite understand but I'm continually fascinated and enchanted by living in the midst of it.

Each spring, every fallen log on the edge of the lake is covered with tur-tles…great, great granddaddy, who is two feet long and wide, stair-stepped in size down to babies, all emerging from hibernation to bask in the first spring warmth. At night, the bullfrogs and the screech owls return and grace the woods with their night sounds. The deep-throated bass of the frog calling his mate rings through the trees like a foghorn until he finally sleeps just before dawn. The screech owls do just that…screech! And, by July, the cicadas and crickets are singing their song in the trees each and every night and the lightning bugs twinkle to add a mystical touch.

The geese fly in every evening at dusk, in formation, and splash into the lake to settle down for the night. They honk and flap their wings. Various kinds of ducks visit us during the winter…mergansers and buffleheads. As spring approaches and turns into summer, I assume they migrate further north and I'll see them again migrating south during fall and winter months. We always seem to have a fair number of mallards raise their young and stay all year long.

In addition, every year the lake gets a new beaver or two; this year we have a muskrat. I've seen red fox running through the woods, and every year, in early summer, a raccoon or two relishes a midnight meal by draining my bird feeders.

I know that hunting and fishing are a way of life in many parts of the country, but it definitely isn't a norm in Southern California. It's amazing to me that I lived there for forty-four years and never knew anyone who owned a gun. I've found that it's unusual if you encounter a native Georgian or Southerner who doesn't own several. Hunting and fishing are BIG in Georgia.

Along with the love of hunting and fishing, Southerners also have a healthy respect and appreciation for maintaining their natural resources. Most of the folks I know who participate in these sports also belong to organizations to protect the habitats where these game animals and waterfowl reside. Much time, money, and effort is donated to the preservation of wildlife, the lakes, the rivers, and the forests so that generations to come can enjoy and marvel at the natural world. Animals are killed as much for sport as they are for the meat or to cull the herds. If too many animals are in the herd, the forest cannot sustain them. They'd ultimately die from starvation and disease without Georgia's hunters thinning their numbers each year. The fishermen work to keep the waterways clean and clear so that the fish can spawn and multiply. They all provide a service that helps maintain a way of life that's connected to the natural world and grounds the human spirit.

To Southerners, these rank among the important things in life.

—Think I'll Stay Awhile!—

Living in the South has grounded me in a way that I never anticipated when I first moved here. I had no clear understanding of the weather or seasons and how they affect the cycle of life. Georgia has shown me that winter is for resting and recharging one's inner batteries; spring is the rebirth and the prelude to the summer of tremendous growth and fall…fall is the time to harvest and celebrate the abundance that Mother Earth provides us all before we settle down, once again, to repeat the cycle, year after year. This cycle renews my spirit and makes my life healthy and whole.

The people of the South have taught me to slow down and realize that your daily relationships to people and nature are what life is about…not hustle, bustle, hurry, scurry or the accumulation of material things.

I'll continue to putter in my garden, drink sweet tea, eat an occasional meal at the Waffle House, and watch, with magical wonder, all the wildlife that fills my daily life and greatly appreciate the Southern hospitality, friendliness, and lifestyle. Pray that urban sprawl does not destroy all that is unique, gracious, and wonderful about making a home in the northern Atlanta suburbs.

An Afternoon Off

By Terry Baddoo

Framed in the rear-view mirror, Atlanta receded into the smog as he blazed his way up I-85 in the midday sun. Sacked; whacked; axed; cut; iced; booted; terminated. He'd been trying each one for size since the Connector, and not one did justice to the deep sense of loss and anger that weighed on his chest like a coronary.

Stepping harder on the gas, he merged onto Georgia 400, tailgating a minivan with Soccer Mom stickers on the back, before juicing his Beemer and switching lanes, casting a look of disdain as he passed. Cutting back outside to avoid the line of cars exiting for Lenox Mall, he powered on through the toll plaza, flipping the bird at the "Thank You" sign for being so cheery.

This wasn't supposed to happen, not to him. He was Jon Smith. He'd sold his soul for a corner office and considered himself an untouchable—the firer, not the firee. Yet, on Manic Monday, he'd been canned with the other grunts by a director of human resources with a fake British accent who was young enough to be his son.

It hadn't been pretty. In a more rational moment, he wouldn't have shot the messenger. But the rough justice defied rationale, so he let him have it. Unloading a scatter-gun of curses that brought others running to witness the carnage as the DHR recoiled.

Striding down the Green Mile seconds after sentencing he felt betrayed—a feeling that wasn't relieved by a right hook to the dry wall or a foot through the face of B.J. Perryman, the CEO whose portrait he'd yanked from its mount and ventilated. Security was summoned, but came on the elevator while he took the stairs for a slower fall from grace.

Down in the lobby, he barged past the suited and booted offensive line without apology. He felt like a bum, unwanted and unworthy, and he just wanted to kick the shit out of the whole world.

Out on Peachtree he looked up, leaning back to see the Stars and Stripes hanging limp atop the building he'd called "work" since the Reagan era. He'd been part of the foundations, or so he'd thought. One of the pillars. But now, as a man among the masses, he was on the outside looking in, as his past replayed on the plate glass windows like a home movie.

The long hours behind the revolving doors had paid for the fabric of his adult life. For the rent on his bachelor pad in Buckhead; drinks at the Hyatt where he'd first met Suzy; the ring that had sealed the deal in Piedmont Park; the five-bedroom exile in Alpharetta; Braves season tickets for him and the boys; the Hilton Head condo; seats at Chastain; Botox! The list went on and on. His things, he'd believed. But now, as he took the exit lane for Mansell Road, he realized they'd all been company property.

With the kids at school and Suzy at Spa Sydell, booked solid with the Windward ladies who lunch, he decided home would be too solitary. He wasn't quite suicidal, but he wasn't much of a gambler either, and didn't want to tempt fate. So, instead of going straight, he abruptly swung over to the left, incurring the wrath of a boy racer in a souped-up Honda Civic who didn't know what he was messing with.

Just beating the lights, he turned onto North Point Parkway, past the Smokey Bones barbecue joint and then immediately right into the parking lot of the AMC Mansell Crossing. The lot was close to empty. And, as he chose a space, he wondered why the theater stayed open with more staff than patrons. Still, he was grateful for the diversion, and scanned the list of movies looking for some R-rated violence.

Inside, the theater was cool and sterile. The cloying smell of popcorn and artificial butter doing nothing to enhance the sense of community in the solitary afternoon wilderness. To him, only sad sacks were alone at the movies at this hour: the friendless, the old, and the unemployed. And as he took his seat with a Diet Coke, and a bucketful of bitterness, he hated himself.

The movie was a clunker—a *Die Hard* rip-off with a wrestler in the lead and special effects that blew the cast off the screen. What dialogue there was had mostly been submerged under the soundtrack, though he had the benefit of hearing every line repeated by an old geezer two rows down who played every part. It didn't matter though, he was barely watching. And, after an hour or so, he quit, leaving the hero dangling ninety floors up in a crumbling ivory tower.

When his eyes adjusted to the sunlight, he opened his Blackberry and checked for messages. Nada. Even the spammers had deemed him redundant. He turned it off, along with his cell, and looked at his Rolex, one-ten. What now?

Wandering over to Starbucks on the corner of Barnes & Noble, he pushed through the glass door and joined the line of drones seeking a lift at the butt end of their lunch breaks. A few hours ago he'd have fitted right in, with people to see and deals to be done. But now he felt like a fraud, and yanked off his tie before reaching the register.

Ordering a tall triple-shot latte, he gave his name and moved to the end counter, staring vacantly as the black-clad barista did her thing with coffee, milk and steam. Had this really happened? Or would he wake up with a start any minute, slumped in his den with his glasses askew and the *New York Times* open on his chest? It couldn't be over, could it? Not for him, with share options and a reserved parking space. "Work to live," that was his dinner party mantra. But he didn't subscribe to it. A man is defined by his job, that's what he really believed. You are what you do. And if you do nothing? Well, he didn't need to finish that thought, did he?

A minute later, the barista interrupted his flow, just as he realized what he should have said to the DHR. Like the coffee, it was pithy and caustic. The Hope Diamond of comebacks. It wouldn't have saved his job, but at least he'd have gone down in a blaze of glory instead of a tsunami of spittle.

Sipping his drink in its a cardboard cup-holder, he turned and went through the security screen into the bookstore. He wasn't a frequent customer, not like the browsers he saw when he whipped in for his *Time* or *Sports Illustrated*. They were moochers in his eyes, malingerers with nothing better to do. He'd bought the odd book, mainly for Suzy or the boys, but he'd never been given to spending much time in the place. Things to do. But not today.

Bypassing the shelves of chick-lit with their kaleidoscope covers, he wandered up and down the Fiction & Literature aisles, pecking and poking at the odd title that caught his eye. Reading the blurbs, he was amazed at how many novels were focused on crime. Murder, abduction, rape, extortion—the literary world was a dangerous place to live. Every other hero was a cop or a lawyer, and those that weren't were in forensics, plucking crucial clues from bodily fluids like subatomic fisherman. That was a job he could do, given the training. He wasn't squeamish. He'd been the go-to guy when it came to diaper duty, and mopped up more than his fair share of vomit when the boys were sick. Besides, wading around in other people's mess was what he'd done all his working life. He was a troubleshooter, a fixer of problems, a finder of solutions.

After a brief stop in Self-Help, where he helped himself to a couple of books about cheese and colored parachutes, he paid and left. two-fifteen, still too early to head home. Back in his car, he turned right along North Point Parkway, and left by Wachovia heading for the mall. Taking the ring road, he circled the vast lot, then parked outside Macy's, which he still called Rich's because he disliked change.

He was a reluctant shopper, and secretly longed for the days when Levis and a clean t-shirt constituted his "wardrobe." Most of all, he hated department stores, which he didn't quite trust. Their incessant sales and money-off coupons in the weekend AJC felt like he was being sucker punched into avarice. Like it was all a ruse to mug the innocents every Hallmark holiday. He'd often threatened to get involved at the Chamber of Commerce, get the spurious promotions banned. He had the contacts via the Masons. Today north Fulton, tomorrow the world. But who was he kidding? He was out of that league now, part of the rank-and-file, and might never have the power again.

Once in the store, he made straight for the escalator, riding up behind a perky blonde teen in a crop-top and cargo pants who was talking on one phone while texting on another. Her thumb strafed the keys like a court stenographer, while the barrage of girlie chatter never let up. This was multi-tasking on a virtuoso level, he thought. But, as he reached the top and saw her clone doing the same, he realized he was wrong. These were the tomorrow people, part of the new world order, and they made him feel obsolete.

Shirts. Some new shirts might cheer him up. Crisp, pinned and folded, they'd never look as good as they did now. The virgin cloth all gussied up in shiny cellophane that crackled to the touch. His shopping aversion meant he normally bought a dozen at a time, replacing one batch with another every six months and giving the old ones to Suzy, who drove them up to Goodwill on Alpharetta Highway.

Sifting through the racks, he had no brand loyalty, choosing shirts by color and pattern. And since Messrs. Hilfiger, Van Heusen, Klein and the rest each measured a 16-inch collar differently, he headed to the changing room to try them on, pausing briefly to grab a handful of ties that might complement.

He chose the stall with wheelchair access giving him more room to pose and strut. He doubted the disabled used it much anyway, and took it for a statutory requirement. Laying his selections on the bench, he opted for a blue-checked Hilfiger first, with a high collar and French cuffs, which would be perfect with the monogrammed cufflinks he'd chosen for his twentieth anniversary gift from the company. He'd earmarked a solid gold tie-pin for his twenty-fifth next year, but it was now clear he'd been coveting fool's gold.

The shirt had more pins than a bulletin board, and as he carefully removed the two installed to puncture his larynx, he caught sight of himself in the mirror. The light wasn't great, but was his hairline as far back this morning? Did his chin sag quite so much? And was that a paunch on his once slender frame? He stared intently, seeing a middle-aged man. Fat, balding, and now unemployed. How had he got here? It was like he was melting. As if his ice-sculptured life, frozen in time for so long, would soon be a puddle on the floor, to be stepped over and then forgotten as it evaporated into the ether.

"Ouch!"

While lost in himself, he'd let down his guard, allowing a renegade pin, lodged somewhere round the armpit, to stab his finger and burst the bubble of self pity.

What was he doing anyway? he thought, licking off the globule of blood. He didn't need these shirts. He didn't need these ties. This was the uniform of the work force, to which he no longer belonged. He was de-mobbed, discharged, free from obligation.

Free! The word hit him like a taser. And like a perp realizing the gig was up, it also incited more clarity. Tossing the Hilfiger on the bench, he sat down and stared at the carpet, contemplating his new reality. For every action there's an equal and opposite reaction, so they say. So the flipside to corporate confinement must be liberation. What was it he'd learnt at management training, while crossing the Chattahoochee buck naked? See every setback as an opportunity. An opportunity to do better, to learn, to grow, that's what they meant. And that's what this was, a do-over. The DHR had done him a favor, releasing him from the bounds of convention, giving him license to re-invent. He felt like Madonna.

Leaving the shirts and ties where they lay, he strode from the changing room and out of the store towards the mall exit, his eureka moment putting a smile on his face and a bounce in his step. He'd always been prone to mood swings, but this was bi-polar—one word to make him relish the future like Pavlov's dogs.

Jumping into his car, he gunned the engine and switched on XM radio, tuning it to the Sixties channel, where the Stones came blaring from the speakers with classic Jagger in his pomp. The angry old men were still his heroes. He was their biggest closet fan. And, as he turned right onto Haynes Bridge heading for Old Alabama, he continued to sing, long after the last chord had decayed and died.

Through the gates of his subdivision, he cruised the tree-lined streets at half the requisite 20 miles per hour. Ford in his flivver, all well with the world. This was a renaissance, a chance to become what he wanted instead of wanting what he'd become.

Pressing the garage-door-opener as he approached, he glided into his spot between the family Navigator and Suzy's Mercedes Sports. These were the trappings of success that had so successfully trapped him in a lifestyle he no longer needed. Well, it was time to embrace the amnesty. And as he shut the garage door behind him, it felt like closure.

"Jon?" Suzy spoke immediately, as he entered the kitchen from the mud room. "Is that you?"

As he tossed his keys on the counter she came in from the deck, dressed for her evening work-out in blue Lycra, but yet to smudge her make-up with sweat. From the family room he could hear the boys doing battle, conquering the universe before dinner on their PlayStation 3.

"Who were you expecting?" he said, dropping his briefcase and walking towards her, arms outstretched.

"Jon. Is everything all right? Where have you been?" she said, avoiding his lips with a cursory kiss on the cheek.

"What do you mean, where have I been? Where I've always been," he said,

"Then what's this about?" she said, pushing the message button on the answer machine.

"You have one message. Monday, one-fifteen pm."

"Hello, Jon…. It's um, David. David Ensley from HR. I tried to reach your cell but it was turned off. Anyway, er, Jon. I've made a bit of a gaff, I don't mind admitting it. Um, you see, the thing is, I er…well, I fired the wrong Jon Smith this morning. Yes, I know, bit of large one, eh? But you see it was supposed to be Jonathan Smith on the fifth, you know, the VP of Operations? Anyway, cut a long story short, someone made a cock-up with the paperwork and it all came down on you. Sorry about that. Human error, I'm sure you understand? But, er, the good thing is, we want you back, even though technically I suppose you were never really gone in the first place. Anyway, that's as maybe, but er…. So give it some thought, will you? B.J says take a few days off, if you like. Nice little break, eh? I expect you could use it. And, um, give me call me at the end of the week. Let me know…. Better still, just come in Monday morning as usual and we'll say no more about it, eh? Sorry again, Jon. And, er, no hard feelings, okay? Have a nice afternoon."

High School Graduation

By Jordan Segal

My heart is racing quickly
As I walk to my last class
I heard the final's tough in there
I pray to God I'll pass.

The tardy bell starts ringing
Just as I step in
"You have until 12:40
Lift your pencils and begin."

I'm filling in my answers
With a sharpened No. 2
I review my years at Roswell High
And all I got to do.

I turn in my last final,
My chin held high and proud
I walk out through the Hornets' doors
My face turned toward the crowd.

There's water in my toes
Moving upward toward my feet
It's rushing up my thighs
As I leave my seat.

I'm in Ray Manus Stadium
With diploma, cap, and gown;
The tears are finally to my eyes
The first drop hits the ground.

The Gaffe of the Magi

By George Weinstein

A buck twenty-two. That was all. And all of it was in pennies, nickels and dimes, the denominations no one bothered to carry around anymore. You've seen people emptying their pockets of these weighty nuisances on the street corner, as if it would make the difference between life and death when they crossed against the traffic. Perhaps you have done so yourself, to lighten your load or make room for something worth carrying about. Well, to Jim, living on the streets, these were worth stooping over to acquire. He greeted each Lincoln, Jefferson and FDR with a smile and imagined their profiles beaming back as he rescued them from one of the sidewalks that grace fair Alpharetta. He shined up each one on the filthy, frayed forearms of his worn jacket. Jim and the coat were much too thin for the encroaching winter. He counted out his life savings for a third time as busy, warmly wrapped shoppers jostled him. One hundred and twenty-two cents. And tomorrow would be Christmas Day.

Christmas Day to Jim Young did not mean carols and holiday feasting, evergreens festooned with electric lights and spun glass. To Jim Young, this December 25th could mark his entry into high society. It was the day when Mr. and Mrs. Magus invited into their opulent home all of the very best young men in town. Jim just knew he belonged to that set. Once inside that gorgeous pile, he'd instantly absorb the wisdom derived from their education, the manners distilled from their refinement, and the opportunities accrued from their connections. No invitation was needed to enter the Magus home. Rather, Mr. Magus posted himself as sentinel at his grand front door and judged each prospective reveler, and the gift proffered, through the flashing lens of his monocle, a nod or a sniff respectively welcoming or condemning that individual.

In his previous attempts at entrance, Master James Young was rebuffed with a curt inhalation. Jim blamed this on his shabby clothes and the unkempt hair upon his crown and chin. In addition, the gifts he selected were those previously rejected by others in the direction of the cavernous dumpsters that hulked behind the North Point Mall. He credited Mr. Magus's excellent breeding for dismissing such obvious, albeit sincere, riffraff as he.

Life on the streets was taking its toll on poor Jim and he inferred from the untimely deaths of many of his peers that, very likely, he would not live to see another anniversary of the Babe's birth. It was now or never, Jim decided. But how much could he improve himself with just a buck twenty-two in hand?

It was then that Fate blew in, or, rather, Fate blew the broadsheet of newsprint against Jim's ankle. He picked it up and looked for the nearest trashcan. As a resident of the sidewalks, it was his intention to keep them clean. On the way to the sanitation cylinder, he glanced down at the page from the *AJC* and saw on one side the editorials. His favorite columnist, Walter L. Winch, was heralding the grand opening of Plasma Plus, the cutting-edge organ bank that paid cash for extraneous and redundant hardware. Jim summed the figures that Winch quoted and saw his opportunity.

The Plasma Plus people were delighted to relieve him of the organic equivalent of so many pennies, nickels, and dimes, paying him in gorgeous green gelt, to the tune of ten Benjamin Franklins. They were quite efficient and when the Krazy Glue dried and the anesthetic wore off, Jim still had an evening left to indulge himself in an orgy of haberdasheries, grooming salons, and tony shops, the best Alpharetta had to offer. Nine Franklins, a Grant, a Jackson, and a Hamilton later, he had just enough to treat himself to eight hours of repose at the No-Tell Motel, investing all but twenty-two of his original pennies on indoor slumber so he wouldn't wrinkle his clothes nor lose his gift.

Jim arose with an early wakeup call: two working ladies exchanging gunfire, grenades, and great imprecations below his window. He showered and rubbed himself vigorously with the towel that was rather similar in most respects to the lucky *AJC* broadsheet that had clung to his leg the day before. It was amazing that no scars sullied his form, front or back, just as Plasma Plus promised. He combed his hair and studied his profile, marveling at the sight of a jaw and lip free from that which only waved and curled stylishly upon his crown. Dressing in the crisp tuxedo and lacing up exquisitely cobbled shoes, Jim already felt himself a new and better man. He slid the slim, elegantly wrapped package into his interior breast pocket, enveloped his shoulders in a heavy wool overcoat and decided to abandon the tattered rags of his previous life upon the threadbare carpet. A clean break.

The women on the sidewalk ceased their gunplay and even sweetened their voices and language when they saw Jim emerge, Fred Astaire stepping off the silver screen and onto their disputed block of concrete. They called to him with honeyed pipes and displayed enough of their persons that the Plasma Plus people would have salivated had they been about at a quarter-past-six on Christmas morning. Jim accepted their attention as discriminate evidence of his swank new self.

Besides other civil and uncivil servants of the public, eager to provide Christmas cheer on a sliding scale of remuneration, Jim encountered no one on his stroll across town. He arrived at the Windward Haven address of Mr. Silas

Claudius Magus just in time to join the line of initial applicants. Jim's long walk supplied a hearty ruddiness to his cheeks, which had been rather pale from the transaction of twenty hours before. He admired the smartly attired, expensively coiffed strangers—"peers" he corrected himself—who marched up the pink Tuscan marble stairs, evergreen garlands coiling up the balustrades on either side like snakes made of money.

Jim recalled his previous failures to pass muster, as if reviewing a documentary of someone else's pitiful life, while feeling supremely confident in the outcome immediately to follow. He heard the haughty intake of air and saw the monocle flash sideways like Poe's pendulum as the fellow in front of him was sent on his way. Jim felt a slight trickle of doubt, a single, cold drop of sweat slicing down his spine, as he realized that not one of the first twenty acolytes was granted access to the stately manse. Ultimately undaunted, he held himself even straighter and cast his features in the arrogant sneer of entitlement worn by Mr. Magus himself as he stepped up to the great man. The likeness must have been uncanny, for the gentleman looked him over with utmost care, as you may have done yourself with the two-year-olds at the Wills Road horse auctions.

The forgotten monocle dangled and swayed as did Jim's spirits under such close scrutiny. With a casualness that he no longer felt, Jim reached within his coat and tuxedo jacket and withdrew the gift. Silas Claudius Magus paused and accepted the slender package, a manicured nail slicing through the foil wrapping like a raptor's talon through a Christmas goose. He lifted off the cover and extracted the gilt-edged pince-nez with a pale thumb and forefinger.

An audible sigh escaped his patrician lips. He dropped the box in his eagerness to expand the space between the lenses and insert his nose betwixt them. Silas Claudius Magus peered through the twin flashing prisms, his crystalline blue eyes swirling like hurricanes as tears moistened them. He gave an emphatic nod to Jim and as the aristocrat-to-be made his victorious entrance through the mammoth doorway, he heard Mr. Magus utter two syllables that sent the queue of supplicants scattering like gaily dressed pigeons: "No more."

Jim turned to watch his mentor stride toward him. A hitherto invisible servant sidled forward and closed the mahogany gates with a resounding boom. Silas Claudius Magus actually put his arm around Jim Young's shoulders. It was the man's words, though, that elevated Jim to a rarified plane: "Welcome home, my boy."

"Thank you, sir," Jim said, his features betraying briefly the astonishment that seemed to raise every follicle on his head by an inch.

Mr. Magus said to the butler who was blending once more into the shadows, "Make the preparations." He then looked at Jim with his enhanced orbs and explained, as he guided him through the cavernous rooms, "Your timing was a gift from God. For years we have been inviting the very finest young men, searching for our own savior on this anniversary of His birth. We were afraid that poor Della wouldn't see another Christmas Day after this one." He led Jim down a flight of wide stone steps. A familiar scent tickled Jim's nose, but he could not place it as he gaped at the enormous suite into which they descended. A woman of Jim's age was propped up in a gigantic bed by a score of satin pillows. She looked pale and wan, much like Jim did before his shopping spree. In fact, as Jim was drawn closer to her, he thought their resemblance was rather remarkable. A middle-aged woman sat beside her, holding her hand. She appraised Jim and nodded.

The great man adjusted the lenses on his proboscis and announced, "Della, Mary, I've found him. Son, what is your given name?"

"James Dillingham Young," Jim replied. In truth, he had no middle name, but he saw the moniker on a letterbox somewhere and it appealed to him.

"Well, James Dillingham Young, meet Della Claudette Magus, your twin sister, and Mary Margaret Magus, your mother."

Jim nearly bit through his tongue. "Excuse me, sir, there must be some mistake. I'm here to gain a foothold in the upper crust, to absorb your superior ways and launch myself into the stratosphere of society. I have no sister and, with all due respect to you, ma'am, I already have a mother."

The great man slapped him affectionately on the back. "Nonsense, son! I'll tell you a story. Every family has a few skeletons. In our case, we started out from humble backgrounds, Mary and I, didn't we, dear?"

"Yes, indeed," she pronounced, patting Della's hand, "and thank goodness that shameful water is well under the bridge."

Mr. Magus continued, "Mary had fraternal twins a year into our marriage and we knew we could only support one. We decided to flip a coin, which, alas, was a mere penny in our case, something I wouldn't weigh down my pockets with now. Heads to keep the girl, tails to keep the boy. I still remember honest Abe's beaming profile in the palm of my hand. Our son was put up for adoption that very day. And now here you are, looking as refined as if we'd raised you ourselves."

"But, sir, my parents never said I was adopted."

"Of course they didn't, James," came the reply. "Who would tell their child such a dreadful thing?"

Della spoke up, still just a whisper, "Perhaps a blood test, just to be sure."

"Why, I am sure!" the magnate said. "I can see it with my own eyes, especially after James here gave me these wonderful specs. This monocle is a child's toy next to them." He yanked the silk ribbon off his jacket, the button that held it flying off and striking Jim in the forehead. Mr. Magus dropped the single lens and ground it under his foot. He tapped the pince-nez, canting it leeward, "When I put these on, it was so clear. The prodigal son returneth!"

Mrs. Magus patted Della's hand some more. "I agree with your father, precious. One could not be more sure. It is the ultimate Christmas present."

The butler opened a door at the end of the room, displaying a glowing white chamber with fantastical lights and the chiming, beeping and chirping of veritable carols. "Ready, sir," the butler intoned.

Mr. Magus took Jim by the shoulder again and propelled him toward the gleaming room. "What was that you were saying about entering our superior circle? Of course, my boy, of course. You're part of the family, reunited with your sister and your natural parents. It's not a 'foothold' Della needs, though. We're aiming at something a little higher."

Jim saw two beds on chrome racks, side by side, and figures clad head-to-toe in jade green moving back and forth with the alacrity of Santa's elves on the 24th.

Jim sniffed again as three green-clad figures approached him. Alcohol, he thought. Disinfectant. He turned, but there was the implacable Mr. Magus, beaming behind his skewed lenses. Beyond the man's shoulder, Jim could see the butler and Mrs. Magus assisting Della into a wheelchair.

"Hurry now, son, off with the coat and dinner jacket. We'll have lots of fine clothes waiting for you when you come to."

"'Come to'?" Jim shouted as gloved hands drew him backward. "I'm not going anywhere!"

Silas Claudius Magus laughed, his belly shaking like a bowl full of blood pudding. "Just into the next room. Della needs your help, James. Consider it your Christmas present to her.

"She requires a kidney with a perfect match. She's lost one and the other is about to give up the ghost. Why that look on your face, James? Everybody has a spare."

Humming Bird Call

By Marre Dangar Stevens

Each Spring she dreams her siren's song,

Although she cannot hear.

In dark earth she plants her music.

Flames of salvia flamenco strings.

Scarlet deep throated petunias

Pounding out their heavy fragrance.

Sunset painted pentas

Playing pizzicato riffs,

To the emerald mysteries.

In deep summer's long hot days

They see her song.

In their iridescent flight they come,

Dancing to her silent tarantella.

The Package

By Walter Lawrence

The morning's downpour had washed away most of the thicker grime from the streets and sidewalks, but their pock-marked surfaces remained fairly gritty. The puddles were slick thin oil sheens.

Roger Beckman was lost.

Well, not exactly lost. After all, Roswell, Georgia was his home town. But, it had been more than a decade since he had been to Five Points in downtown Atlanta. As he often told friends, "I don't see any reason to go south of the river," meaning the muddy Chattahoochee that demarcated the city from the northern suburbs. The cab had dropped him off at the big park near the Flatiron Building, because he wanted to look around some of the places he had regularly frequented so long ago. He recognized none of them in more than a vague way. So much had changed.

He shrugged and made his way to Houston Street. It too had that now-unfamiliar-look, but fortunately Houston was only three blocks long. The address to the Morgan Literary Group was number 225, the middle of the block. Roger guessed it to be the old three-story brick building. No exterior signage adorned the aged red walls, so Roger bounded up the stairs and through the massive entry doors to look for a building directory. The office he was looking for occupied part of the third floor.

Morgan Literary was housed in a large suite at the north end of the building. The receptionist's console was a substantial structure made of some expensive dark wood, all but hiding the pleasant but bluntly professional keeper-of-all-access. Something in her look told all who entered that she had heard it all before.

Roger began to panic. It wasn't as if he had an actual appointment to see anyone. This was going to have to be all wit and charm, and most likely some quick finesse, if he could muster it.

"Hi." He began, looking around to possibly spot the name on the door of the man he was looking for. He didn't see it.

"May I help you?" was her pleasant reply.

"Sure. I've gotta package here for Dennis Morgan. He asked me to bring it to him today." The last part was a gallant lie at best. Lying was permitted he told himself. He was, after all, a fiction writer.

"Just leave it with me, and I'll see that he gets it."

She reached for the package, but could only grab an edge. Roger had taken a small step back—winning the polite wrestling match.

"Well, actually I'd like to give to him myself. Ya know, put a face to the voice on the phone. Shake his hand, start the bonding. Give him my first born. The usual stuff."

It worked. A smile began at the corners of her mouth, and her eyes flashed a slight twinkle. She withdrew the reach.

"Sorry, I didn't properly introduce myself. I'm Roger Beckman. Aspiring writer." He stuck out *his* hand, which she shook with polite warmth. "I have a fair amount of talent, and a whole lot of enthusiasm. Am I yammering here?"

She laughed, "Yes, a bit. But it's very disarming. I'm Marie Valdermont."

Roger's eyes widened in sheer delight.

"Valdermont, as in the little town in the upper French Alps, which translates into *decent from the mountain?*"

"Why yes, my father's people are from that part of France. How did you know all that?"

"Oh, names are a huge hobby of mine. In fact, creating new character names is my idea of fun. So, I usually study any names that are new to me. Valdermont was one. I think I saw it in some movie credits."

"O.K., O.K., you've won me over. A little bit. Mr. Morgan is at lunch right now, but he should be back any minute."

"Lunch? It's only ten-thirty. Places that crowded downtown nowadays?"

She laughed again, "No, he's hand holding a nervous client at the donut shop downstairs. He'll probably bring something back with him. Any time now. You can wait right over there. I'll introduce you to him when he comes in." She smiled again, her eyes softening as she gazed directly into his. "What's your book about anyway?"

Roger brightened. He loved to talk about his work. "It's called *Death Takes the Cake*. A mystery set during the thirties in rural Alpharetta. The main character is a guy who...."

"Wait, don't tell me. Dennis lets me read manuscripts sometimes to get another view. I'll get him to let me see yours."

Roger smiled broadly, now. But he looked at his watch. Time was becoming a factor. He had to be across town soon. His original plan had been for a mere five minute audience with Morgan, and then on to the MARTA station.

Marie picked up on this. "You can leave it. I'll see that he gets it. No, really." She saw the beginnings of doubt cloud his face.

"Well, I'd really like to do it myself. I could come back some other time." But he knew he couldn't miss the meeting he was bound for. It was his livelihood, the one that actually supported his writing career.

Marie looked at him again, waiting for him to finish the argument he was having with himself. "So, what's it going to be? I'll give it to him as soon as he gets in, I promise."

"On two conditions."

"*Conditions?* That's certainly cheeky. Like what?"

"Like you have coffee with me at that Starbucks around the corner, one day next week."

She looked at him like an alert mongoose inspecting a serpent in its path. "O.K., and the other?"

"You give me your home phone number."

"For a man with pretty blue eyes, sir, you are somewhat bold." She credibly feigned a Southern belle's demure indifference. "Let's hope your book is as interesting." She looked at Roger for a long moment, doing some mental calculations based on a logic that requires the double-X chromosome. Finally, she penned something on the back of a business card. "Tuesday, 11:45. One time offer."

Roger handed her the package with glee, taking the card in return. "Tuesday it is. I'll be the one with the big smile." He turned and made his way to the elevators, humming to himself as he walked down the hallway.

He knew Morgan would get the manuscript, probably with some comments from his new friend. It all bode well. Worse case, he'd peddle the work somewhere else. But now at least he had a date with a fascinating woman.

Roger wondered if he would actually get to meet Dennis Morgan one day; perhaps have an artsy writer's lunch with him. That would leave out his favorites, Georgia Pig on Green Street or Southern Skillet on Highway 9. More like Mittie's Tea Room just off the Square. No, he'd save the barbeque and the Krispy Kremes for Ms. Valdemont. What Southern gal wouldn't go for that?

He smiled to himself. It never hurt to have an imagination.

His World

By Terry Segal

He lives inside of his body but outside of his mind.

His soul fleets past the translucent blue windows of his eyes and connects with her, like a child peering around the edge of the pane before darting back behind the curtain again.

His smile, now pulled up at the corners by sagging elastic and wound 'round each ear, must have dazzled her back in the day. Dapper, still, with his cap and cane, his long legs unfold as he stands; a new colt in neon green trousers. Did she buy them for him; one shade in her Technicolor palette of tasks each day?

Released from his grip his cane crashes to the ground, thundering like a fallen oak.

He doesn't notice and appears as if he might sprint on legs of fifty years ago.

She moves to him, his balance point. A prisoner of love she is, trapped by her past with this gentle stranger who greets her anew, delighted at his good fortune. As he shuffles off to the solarium to nap, she sighs, alone again, thoughts for one in a mind that is always set for two.

She picks up her brush and paints the world beyond her walls, filled with people and trees, skyscrapers and sunsets. In a burst of movement, she flees from the sleeping giant and leaps into the sailboat that is still wet from the blend of Hunter's Green and Ultramarine. She sails across the sun-dappled waves as she breathes in the fresh air of freedom.

In too short a time though, shadows grow long, the wind changes direction, and she must return. He stirs and she moves to him. But one day, she'll set sail again and glide past the edges of her canvas.

The Great Skin-So-Soft Soapy-Butt Caper

By Buzz Bernard

Sometimes losing is the best revenge. I realized that in high school when I pulled off the Great Skin-So-Soft Soapy-Butt Caper on Billy Breitenhoffer.

Billy was big, surly and stupid and survived his adolescence primarily by intimidation. He wasn't necessarily violent, but he knew how to exude the essence of violence. All he had to do was cock his bowling ball-sized fist in front of your face, drool slightly from the corners of his mouth and call you "needle dick" or "jerk off" and you did or gave him whatever he wanted. He was the antithesis of the other kids I grew up with in north Fulton County. Rumor had it his family had fled the North Carolina mountains after their house blew up. Cooking meth, I guess.

Billy took a particular dislike to me, which I assume was largely inherent because I went out of my way to avoid him. But I couldn't avoid him on the football practice field. There I was his personal tackling dummy. Even in half-speed drills he'd block or tackle me at full speed. In scrimmages, he'd invariably fail to hear the whistle blow at the end of a play and nail me after I'd relaxed my vigilance. At the bottom of a pile, he'd always find a way to grind a fist or cleat into my face. The coaches turned their backs on Billy's excesses. If not their star lineman, he at least filled a huge space on both the offensive and defensive lines. Never mind he didn't know a split infinitive from a split end, or a numerator from an elevator.

At any rate, you can imagine my chagrin one November evening when I found myself marooned in the locker room after practice with Billy and another kid, Ralph Monk. I knew Ralph only vaguely and wasn't sure whether he was one of Billy's henchmen, a neutral observer or potential ally.

I figured I'd find out soon enough, however, since we were going to be stuck in that moist, malodorous prison for at least a couple of hours until the monthly PTA meeting had concluded and our parents could take us home.

The coaches had bailed out quickly to attend the meeting, leaving us three kids with a stern warning to behave ourselves, not leave the showers running and turn out the lights when we left. We took our time undressing, stuffing our rancid socks and jocks into our gym bags—which I suspect were culturing all sorts of exotic microbiotic growth—and throwing our uniforms—so layered in mud they looked like giant Baby Ruth candy bars—into the laundry bin.

It had been a pneumonia-inducing practice in wind-swept rain and temperatures that belonged in New England, not north Georgia. We loitered in the showers for a long time, luxuriating under cascades of steaming water. Yet we still had an hour to kill.

Billy, a towel wound around his 55-gallon-drum-sized midsection, stalked over to me after we'd showered. "Soap up your butt, needle dick," he said. "Time for a little contest." Today such a statement might have sinister sexual overtones, but not back then. I knew what he meant. Simple, idiot fun. Get your rear cheeks as soapy as possible, take a running start and slide full tilt along the wet concrete floor of the locker room on your butt. Long slide wins.

I couldn't refuse, of course. "You in, Ralph?" I asked. Ralph just shrugged and nodded. I decided he wasn't one of Billy's allies.

Billy went first. Buck naked, he hit the floor with a tremendous "splosh" and rocketed toward the far end of the room. He sounded like a battleship cutting a wake through a calm sea. I paced off his slide. "Thirty-one feet," I said. "Not bad."

"My record's thirty-nine," he grumped.

Ralph went next, kicking up a small rooster tail of water as he bested Billy's skid by four feet.

Billy muttered an obscenity, describing something I thought physically impossible, then glared at me. A tacit warning.

Screw you, I thought. And went for it. Lots of soap, a little secret squirt of Skin-So-Soft bath oil (something Mom had slipped into my gym bag), a quick sprint, a nice smooth sit down and I'm PT 109 in shallow water. I was still under power when I whacked solidly into the double doors at the far end of the locker room. Forty feet! Damned if I hadn't just broken Billy's unofficial record.

Ralph was first to greet me. He extended his hand to pull me up. "Nice slide, dork," he whispered. "Should I give you last rites now?" I turned and saw Billy striding toward me, a hairless Sasquatch on the rampage. Bigfoot bent on revenge.

I raised my arms in supplication. "Billy," I said, "that was a test run, just for you. I know how we can get you at least fifty feet."

He stopped and regarded me with suspicious, pinched eyes.

I showed him the bottle of Skin-So-Soft. "With this," I said, "you'll go like a greased pig on ice."

"I can't go no further than you did," he said. He pointed at the doors.

"No problem," I answered. "The doors separate the locker room from the cafeteria. No one's in the cafeteria at night. When you start your slide, Ralph and I will open the doors. You'll get an extra ten feet, I guarantee it."

Billy smiled, lathered up and prepared for his Olympian effort. Ralph and I positioned ourselves on either side of the doors and Billy began his run up. He got a great start and hit the floor with a slap that sounded like a beaver-tail warning. He hurtled madly toward the doors, an albino walrus on a water slide. I nodded to Ralph and we yanked open the portal as Billy knifed past us, on his way to a new soapy-butt slide record. On his way smack-dab into the middle of the November PTA meeting. Naked as the day he was born, but a whole lot cleaner.

His battle cry still rings in my ears. "Oh, shiiiiiiiiittttt."

He transferred to a private school the following week.

May's Biscuits

By Kathleen Craft Boehmig

My grandma, Essie May Brown, used to bake the world's finest southern biscuits, using her own recipe that she'd perfected over decades by the time I, her first grandchild, grew old enough—around toddler-age—to enjoy them. "May's biscuits", as her sisters called them, were soft and creamy inside and crusty on the outside, with enough heft so you could slice them in half and load them down with butter and gravy, and they wouldn't crumble.

My first biscuit was probably soaked with butter and syrup, a favorite Southern treat in the mid-1900s b.c. (before cholesterol). Of course, these days it's physically and politically incorrect to eat yourself into slow coronary suicide in this manner. But you wrap your lips around one of Grandma's biscuits, and you'd beg them to usher the undertaker right on in. Depending on the desired bouquet, you can ladle on honey, pure cane or sorghum (pronounced "sog'um") syrup, or if you're a displaced Yankee, maple syrup or molasses.

Another popular southern treat back then was to slice a biscuit and cover both halves with homemade red-eye gravy. You rarely find this gravy listed on Southern menus anymore. Seems like we'd see it more often. Heck, it's only two ingredients: strong coffee and ham drippin's. Our drippings came from good old cured country ham that we'd hang from the basement rafters, wrapped up tight in layers of cloth to keep varmints out. Grandma would slice up a hunk of that ham real thin, fry it in an iron skillet, mix coffee with the drippings, boil it for a minute or two, put the ham and the gravy over a biscuit hot from the oven, and we'd taste a little bit of heaven.

Any leftover biscuits were saved, and then later sliced in half, buttered and toasted for a delicious snack. These were excellent served with homemade preserves: plum, peach and fig were always my favorites. Hardly anyone puts up preserves now, but some of those new-agey feng-shui fruit spreads are pretty good.

I used to help Grandma with her cooking and baking, and I inherited her Southern way of preparing food. You use a right-smart of some ingredients, a handful of others, and just a little dab of the potent ones like spices and seasonings. Grandma rarely measured anything, and her meals always drew raves.

Grandma died in 1992, and for years I didn't make biscuits. Not due to grief, although I still miss her. But I curtailed my biscuit-making in favor of more healthy eating—still with a Southern flair, but leaning a bit more toward lean meats and steamed vegetables, and less toward pork chops smothered with gravy and vegetables fried with bacon grease. Nowadays I usually serve yeast rolls instead of biscuits.

About ten years ago, though, I was distressed to realize I'd lost Grandma's touch with biscuits. I asked Mom and my aunts about it, but they all used different techniques. I rifled through a few old cookbooks and online recipes without success. The versions in *Mrs. S. R. Dull's Southern Cooking*, a well-used classic I inherited from Grandma, called for too many ingredients. I relegated Grandma's biscuits to a fond, distant memory.

Then, in 2000, Grandma's sister Evy became seriously ill at age ninety-four and was brought to Atlanta for treatment. My mom, her sister Frances and I drove downtown to visit Aunt Evy at the Atlanta Medical Center.

Evy was a quirky, eccentric woman. Passionate, opinionated and loyal like all her siblings, she was as heavy as her twin, Nell, was tiny. Throughout their lives the sisters loved to cook. So did their brother Claude, who started Sconyers Barbeque Restaurant, "the grand old lady of Augusta barbeque." The siblings were never Grandma's equal in the kitchen, but they were all excellent cooks.

The day we visited Aunt Evy in the hospital, the nurse warned us about her dementia. My aunt would be able to sit up and talk with us for only a short time.

She didn't recognize us at first, but after a moment Evy seemed to regain her faculties. We'd brought her a cup of her favorite ice cream—lemon custard—which she accepted gratefully, and we spoke about old times.

"I sure do miss May!" she suddenly exclaimed, her eyes sparkling. "She could make the best biscuits you ever tasted." We all smiled and nodded. She sure could.

"She'd take a right-smart of flour…you know, she always preferred White Lily, but Gold Medal would do." Aunt Evy slurped a big bite of ice cream as I grabbed a pen and began taking notes. We discussed "a right-smart", and interpreted it as approximately two cups.

"Then she'd take some lard—you know, Crisco. She'd reach in the can and get a blob about the size of your fist." My aunt savored another bite of ice cream.

"Once she'd cut that in good, she'd pour in a dab or two of buttermilk. Then she'd roll it out and make the biscuits using her old cookie-cutter with the green han'l'." I was thrilled as I pieced together the recipe. I still had that cookie cutter with the green wooden handle in a kitchen drawer at home.

Aunt Evy's period of lucidity only lasted several minutes, but during that time she related every detail of May's biscuit recipe. Tears welled in my eyes. My culinary birthright had been restored. I tried out the recipe as soon as I got home, and the flavor transported me back to my childhood, to breakfasts in Grandma's sunny kitchen.

I decided to make up a batch of these and take some to Aunt Evy, but I never got the chance. She died on her ninety-fifth birthday, one week after our visit. But that was some parting gift she gave me that day, in between bites of lemon custard ice cream.

I bet they've got great Southern biscuits in heaven nowadays…served with hand-churned butter, red-eye gravy and sorghum syrup. They've certainly got some expert cooks up there.

May's Biscuits
2 cups White Lily self-rising flour (Gold Medal is okay too)
1/3 cup shortening, preferably Crisco
Up to about ¾ cup buttermilk
Preheat your oven to 450 degrees, and put the flour into a large mixing bowl. Add the shortening. Use a manual pastry blender to cut this into the consistency of a coarse meal. Using your hands, mix in the buttermilk—a little bit at a time—until the dough is sticky but not wet, and easily comes off the sides of the bowl. Flour a rolling pin, and roll the dough out to about a half-inch thickness. (Grandma's wooden hand-hewn cutting board was perfect for this, but any smooth, clean, floured surface will do.) Use a cookie-cutter or an upside-down drinking glass dipped in flour to cut out the biscuits. Put them on an ungreased cookie sheet and bake them for 12 to 14 minutes. Slather with butter and any other favorite biscuit condiment, and start checking your cholesterol.

Elfscapade

By George Weinstein

My most harrowing summer job was portraying Ernie, The Keebler Elf, when I was seventeen. I got a call from a temp agency saying it needed someone six feet tall to wear the elf costume at a 4th of July mall appearance in Roswell. I was five-foot-ten, but needed the work enough to lie. At a certain moment in every guy's life, he'll fib and add a couple of inches, usually to get into somewhere he might not otherwise get. My falsehood got me into an eight-foot tall, eighty-pound elf suit <u>outside</u> the mall, where it was 100 degrees for people wearing ventilated clothing. For folks in elf suits it was 125.

I quickly learned there was something worse than sweating in the infernal costume: not being able to see while perspiration soaked me. Ernie had this woven mesh where his throat should be. That was the only source of cooling or visibility and it was almost above my head. When the guys who had the suit helped me into it, they wanted to know if I could see. I wanted to say that I couldn't even breathe.

"How many fingers am I holding up?" one of the dynamic duo asked.

I thought, so much for this job. I could've guessed, figuring most people would hold up two or three. However, the folly of my lie became clear to me, and so I told the truth. My head bowed invisibly in eighty pounds of foam and nylon that could conceal even the most fallen crest. I reported through Ernie's breastbone: "I can't see you holding up any fingers."

"Yeah, that's right. Sorry for the trick question, kid."

So there I was, in the sun, waving blindly at what I assumed were delighted children and amused parents. I did manage to grip the cracker bags I was supposed to be giving away, but didn't know who I was handing them to. I learned if I just stuck out my hand that someone would walk past and take the bag, so it worked, until I figured out that it was the same person standing next to me taking all my crackers.

I swung around to confront the glutton, but my momentum carried me into some poor woman who hit me with her shopping bags. People began shouting and someone pushed me from behind. I was at the center of a small riot, so I did what any self-respecting elf would do.

I ran.

This wasn't such an easy thing in my condition. What saved me was the parking garage that I stumbled into had a height clearance of seven-and-a-half feet and the tip of Ernie's hat was about eight-feet.

Ernie, The Keebler Elf, was decapitated.

At last, I could finally see. No one was chasing me except two little kids who made off with Ernie's head. It's an image that haunts me still.

I made it to my car, climbed out of the suit, stuffed it in the back, and drove past a melee involving twenty adults and an unattended sack of Keebler Town House crackers.

The worst part was that, not only didn't I get paid, but I also had to work two jobs the rest of the summer to reimburse the company $1,000. That was the price on Ernie's head.

Alien Roswell

By John Sheffield

Roswell, Georgia, has silos that sit near the corner of Crabapple and Houze Roads. They have always held a fascination for me, with their domed, phallic symmetry and their grouping. At one time there were five of these structures—today only three remain.

That other Roswell, in New Mexico, also has silos on the nearby Walker Air Force Base. A relic of the cold war, these buried silos were used to house Atlas missiles. They were abandoned in 1965 and one of them was converted into an extraterrestrial communication facility, thus emphasizing the credibility of alien existence and of stories about the crash of an alien spacecraft nearby in the 1947. Government denials that it had alien spacecraft and alien bodies captured the public's imagination, and a tourist industry grew in the area.

The thoughts about silos led me to wonder what our silos contained—only grain?

Prompted by curiosity, I researched them. Apparently, one of our silos had been erected over a stormy period in 1949. Officials FROM Roswell believed that permission for construction had been given by Fulton County. The County believed that it was approved by the city. I suspect that back then planning was haphazard.

A strange feature, visible to passersby, was that this last silo remained gleamingly new and apparently was never used for storage. I heard it suggested that grain production was not sufficient to justify its use. This edifice continued to pique my curiosity and, after the farm was sold around 1983, I decided to investigate.

My favorite time for snooping was early on Sunday mornings: light enough to see detail and early enough that few people were around. I was able only to climb an attached ladder and inspect the outside of the silo. The small door at the bottom remained locked and obstinately immoveable. Other than being cleaner, the exterior of this silo was the same as the others and I began to lose interest.

To be honest, I am not clear what happened on that day I made my last inspection.

"Where are you going?" my wife asked sleepily, as I pulled back the covers and slid my feet to the floor.

"I want to check that silo again."

"I can hear thunder."

"It'll be okay," I replied as I dressed in the semi-dark and went towards the bathroom.

"Your funeral." She turned over and went back to sleep.

She was right. By the time I arrived a violent storm had swept in. I could hear the persistent rumble of thunder and see lightning flashes to the west. I was about to run to my car when I found that the hasp holding the lock on the silo's door had rusted and I was able to force it open and get out of the rain.

I had not brought a flashlight but, fortunately, I had left my pen and pencil protector and laser pointer in my jacket pocket. Behind the door, I came across a plastic curtain which I pushed aside while shining my laser. The thin red beam reflected so brightly that for a moment I was blinded. As my vision cleared, I saw three squat, shiny metal legs facing me. Supported on them, and reaching within a couple of feet of the walls of the silo, was a metal cylinder. The inside of the silo was spotlessly clean and smelled antiseptic, a smell I associate with the arcing products around high voltage electrical equipment.

I made the decision to climb the ladder mounted on the interior wall. My heart was thumping hard and breathing labored as I clambered up to find a fifteen-foot diameter metal sphere resting on the cylinder. By crawling across a metal projection on top of the cylinder I was able to reach the juncture of the cylinder and the sphere on top of it.

The sphere was smooth, with no visible welds or marking of any kind. Its metal felt silky and I rubbed my hand on the part in front of me, nervously pointing the laser beam at the surface. At first I could see only the fun-house-like distorted reflection of my face. But then the reflection looked as if I had gained a tattoo. Faint markings had appeared in a cartouche. The image that came to mind was of the instructions you see painted on aircraft: "Fuel supply," "Not a support," and so on. As I rubbed harder, lightning struck the silo and the markings became clearer. Suddenly, with a pop, a hand-sized door sprung open where I had been rubbing. At the bottom of a cavity was what looked like a button. I could not resist the urge to push the button and plunged my finger in. Nothing happened. I pushed again. Nothing happened. But when I closed the cover, there was a whirring noise from deep inside the main chamber. A generator starting up, I thought as I climbed down and backed away to the door. Suddenly, the smaller sphere rose on a stalk. Simultaneously, a hatch, previously undetectable, opened underneath the main sphere. Tubes pushed down. I ran out and hid behind a tree. Through the driving rain, I saw beams of light shine out of the tubes and the strange craft, in tandem with the silo, rose ever more rapidly into the turbulent clouds and disappeared. But not before a blinding blue light illuminated the area where I was standing, and I fell to the ground. I don't remember how I got home and why I ended up standing in the shower with the water on.

"Are you crazy?" my wife said, opening the shower door.

"It's okay. I was already wet." I continued soaping my clothes, trying to think of a plausible explanation. "It was pouring down out there. I slipped and got mud all over me. It seemed the smartest thing to do."

"You're nuts. I'm going to get some coffee. Want some?'

"Yeah. Thanks." Was I nuts? There wasn't any sign of mud in the shower and my sneakers, though full of water, were clean. I left the wet clothes in the shower, put on a robe and went down to the kitchen.

"If you were outside, you were lucky." A strong emphasis on the "if" showed what my wife believed.

"How so?"

"The local news is all about the tornado that hit near Houze Road this morning."

"It was pretty rough out there,"

"You'll like this." My wife giggled. "The tornado removed one of the silos. Did you see it woosh away?"

A strange coincidence, I wondered. "It must have been after I left." No point in telling her the story I had in my head, I would never have heard the end of it.

Subsequent articles in the papers concluded that the tornado had cleverly extracted only this silo from the group, although reporters acknowledged that it was hard to explain why no pieces had been found. I never told anyone what I saw, but I understood now that it was not only Roswell, New Mexico, that had been visited by aliens. The beings from that planet—with a name that must sound like Roswell—circling another star had also landed here in Georgia. These days, when I meet other original inhabitants of the area I look very closely at them.

Fishing Indoors

By Carolyn Robbins

It was just a funny sound. It came from down the hall. What was it? The Braves were winning and I really didn't want to get up. But it was insistent. It demanded attention.

Was it the fish tank? I rose and walked tentatively towards it. Yes, that was it; the filter and pump had run amuck. I hurried to the computer room where my fish resided. Hoping to get the tank fixed before the next inning started, I flicked the light on and beheld the start of a cascade.

No, it definitely wasn't a filter problem. It was a leak problem. Little fountains of water were spurting from the front. Along the entire five-foot length, rivulets were flowing onto my photo albums sitting snugly underneath on the shelf.

Frantically grabbing albums and flinging them behind me, I yelled to my peacefully sleeping husband, "Get out of bed! We have a flood. I need your help. Get me buckets!"

I kept pulling at my soggy memories, expecting a husband with buckets. A slippery vacation in the West thudded on the floor behind me. Out came last fall's Bermuda trip with a squish. I silently prayed that my daughter's wedding album would be just slightly damp. They all went behind me in a heap. No husband, no help arrived. I glanced at the tank. The fish looked mildly confused that their pond was shrinking. A new stream of water hit me square in the face. Where was he?

I needed buckets and to find some way to disconnect the pump.

I yelled, "Please get up. I need your help. Now!"

No answer. I groaned. Running to laundry room I grabbed three buckets, pivoted and raced back to my flood. Jamming them onto the empty portion of the shelf, the plunks and splats calmed me.

I eyed the power strip sitting on the eight remaining albums. There looked to be a dry spot on the cord where I could grab it.

"Yeow!"

Wrong, it wasn't dry, but the plug pulled from the wall. A miracle, my husband appeared in the doorway. My hero was dressed. Was he afraid to let the fish see him naked?

He looked at me bleary-eyed. "What a mess. What do you want me to do?"

"Get me buckets!" I demanded. Then I added, "From the basement. I already have the upstairs ones."

The water was coming out faster. Now that the whole shelf was finally cleared, I jockeyed the pails under the strongest torrent. But there were still several spurts merrily splashing on the floor. The carpet under my knees squished with every move I took. It seemed like he had left quite a while ago. How long could it take to get buckets?

A yell from the basement, "What are you going to do with the fish?"

"I'm thinking about that. Where are my buckets?"

I eyed my poor fish swimming closer to the bottom of the tank. Where would I put them? The eighteen-inch long bottom feeder was longer than my buckets were round.

My husband arrived at last bearing every known bucket in the house. The dear man is always so thorough. I was so wet. Well, now I had buckets to spare.

He also had more bad news, "Water is now seeping through the floor and it's dripping on your car in the garage. Why did you leave the car windows open?"

"I wasn't expecting it to rain in the garage."

Finally, each stream had its own bucket. The room resounded with various pitched splashes.

"Get the storage box on the right-hand side of the shelf next to the flowerpots. I just remembered it's empty."

Minutes passed and I decided to save the little fish while I was waiting for the box. Plunk, plunk, the little ones went into one of the many buckets of water that were filling under the tank. It was time to move the bottom feeders. I had called one Pleccy because I could never pronounce plecostomus, and Rocky was the eighteen-inch one.

Watching me chase Pleccy with the net, my husband suggested, "Why don't you try using a dishtowel to get him if the net doesn't work." Yawning he said, "Since you seem to have everything under control, I'm going back to bed."

I restrained myself from yelling "coward." Of course the net didn't work. Pleccy angrily flipped his tail, slapped the remaining water, and droplets fell from my face. Sputtering, I trudged once again to the kitchen to get the suggested dishtowel.

With Pleccy, the dishtowel method worked, but Rocky was another matter entirely. I tried to slide it under him. He evaded me. I struggled to lay it flat in the opposite end of the tank and then herd him over it. He stormed it like a bulldozer, wadding it up into a ball at the end of the tank. The water now barely covered him. I reached in and tried to pick him up. Ow! Rocky felt rocky. First I had been electrocuted, and now my fish was stabbing me. By this time Rocky was panicked. He furiously thrashed from one end of the tank to the other. Finally he stopped splashing. I drew a deep breath, plunged my hand into the tank and quickly grabbed him around his tail. Ignoring his stabbing prickles and panicked writhing, I tossed him into the waiting box. For a moment the box rocked from side to side as two very frightened fish crashed into one another, not understanding that I was trying to save their lives. Slowly they settled down, realizing they were just old buddies in a new place.

At about 2:00 a.m., I left the room. I had carefully laid out all the photo albums to dry and emptied all the buckets. I was exhausted. Tomorrow I would figure out what to do with my homeless fish. As I slid into the bed next to my sleeping husband, only one thought crossed my mind: I wonder if the Braves won.

McFarland Road

By Ann Foskey

When I was out in the gray-lit night,
moving slowly through the tall grass that smelled of horses,
I could see the dark tree line
and the mist that covered the earth from the field to the sky.

The moon was under the same blanket,
seeing it all with the same innocent eyes,
tilted, not yet full,
moving, but not knowing
by what familiar force.

Lightning flashed in sheets
and beads of rain fell from the sky
as if to send a message from its source
to touch me, cool me, wake me—
perhaps I was a reflection in its eye.

In the darkness
a deer wandered by,
quiet and alone,
nothing but a rustle
as she browsed.

A brown bat flapped
its wet-leather wings
working the night shift
over the flattened field,
ridding the world of small things
that pester and bite
and chase us from places we would like to be.

The earth was awake with a sleep-like breathing
and all was woven together,
and at the same time weaving.

An owl leapt from its perch and crossed the field,
drawing the covers across the night—
a soft, silent witness gliding through the mist
taking its secrets to its nest.

Joe

By Dodge Lewis

Joe had a special ability.

We didn't realize this right away. Later on, somebody suggested that maybe he was autistic, but nobody really knew.

One Saturday I caught a glimpse of his special ability. I don't know why I hadn't noticed it before. Joe had wanted me to drive him to a Best Buy to look at plasma TVs. I picked him up at his house. Actually, it wasn't his house. The house belonged to his brother, who was in Europe. Joe had turned up with his son the day after his brother had left, and said he was house sitting.

Unlike his brother, Joe didn't have a lot of money himself, but he had made up his mind that his son should have a plasma TV. At Best Buy, we found that the TVs were too expensive, and Joe seemed disappointed and depressed. But the store was having a contest, with a plasma TV as the first prize. I told him to enter the contest. Maybe he would be lucky. He didn't seem at all interested. He looked so down that I practically had to force him to put his name in the contest box just to try to cheer him up. It didn't help though, and he was silent all the way home. He had really wanted that TV for his son.

Anyway, something was niggling at the back of my mind, and I suddenly realized what it was. During the week, I like to work while I'm driving. I carry a portable office I can keep in my lap and work at the red lights. The few minutes at each light add up, and I had gotten good at quickly switching from working to driving when the lights turned green. Something about the drive over on that Saturday seemed odd. Something was different. I paid attention on the way back, and I noticed that we never hit any red lights. Not any. I started counting them. We drove through more than nineteen lights that were all green, and that seemed strange. I said so to Joe.

"Joe, we hit every light green. Do you know what the chances of that are?"

"I don't like to sit at red lights," was all he said.

"What are you telling me? That you changed them all green?" I laughed.

"No. I wished once that I didn't have to sit at red lights. Now I don't."

"Yeah? Do you actually believe that?"

"Yes," he said simply.

"Then why don't you wish for that TV they're giving away?"

"Yeah," he said, perking up, "I wish I could win that TV."

"Right," I said, looking sideways at him. Now he seemed happy.

I met my neighbor Mark at the clubhouse the next day and told him about it, and he said he had noticed some odd stuff too, but thought it was just coincidence. He said he remembered that on several occasions, when Joe was with him, people would pull out of parking places right in front of stores, leaving the best parking spaces free. And it happened more than once.

At this point John came in, lugging his golf bag, and we all three started talking about it. I had gotten to know John pretty well in the two months he had been in the neighborhood. As senior engineering managers, we had a lot in common. John scoffed at what we were saying, and told me I shouldn't even be thinking such nonsense.

"You're an engineer," he said.

"Statistically, I don't think it's reasonable," I said, "to have every light turn green twenty something times in a row. That kind of coincidence is a real stretch."

"So what are you suggesting?" he asked.

"Just that it was unusual," I said, a little embarrassed. I hoped I hadn't said too much, since I knew that Joe and John were good friends. They had known each other for a long time, John had said once. In fact, it had been Joe who had introduced us all to John.

The next day it seemed silly to think it was anything but coincidence and I forgot all about it. Until the next Friday.

I was driving home from work when the traffic slowed almost to a stop on Windward Parkway. I wondered what had happened since it was too early for the really bad rush hour traffic. Then I saw what it was. In front of me was a four car pile-up. As I finally pulled around the wreck, I saw Joe standing there with some people. He was out in the road, almost in danger of being hit by traffic. Then I saw that his car was part of the wreck. I pulled off, parked and hurried back to ask Joe if he was OK.

"Yeah," was all he would say.

"Well, get out of the traffic, Joe," I said, pulling him over to the embankment.

I looked at the wreck, and suddenly realized that Joe's car didn't have a scratch on it. The other cars had somehow collided and jackknifed in some weird choreography of destruction that folded them around Joe's car without ever touching it. I couldn't believe what I was looking at. This didn't seem like any damned coincidence, I thought. That guy is too lucky by far. I knew I shouldn't be thinking that, but I couldn't help it.

We lived in a gated golf community, and were on the course much of our free time. That afternoon I talked to John and Mark again in the clubhouse as we waited for Tony, my other neighbor, to complete the foursome. John was skeptical, of course.

"It was the damnedest thing to see his car sitting there in the middle of a wreck without a scratch on it, and all the other cars totaled," I was saying.

"Maybe you're remembering it that way because you have a preconceived idea. Do you have an actual photograph of the wreck?" John asked.

"Of course not."

"Did anybody else see this miracle?"

"It happened just the way I've described it. My observations are accurate."

"What I'm saying is that it might seem as though his car wasn't touched."

"You're pissing me off," I said.

"Maybe he's lucky because he's autistic," said Mark.

"What?" said John. "What has autism got to do with it? We don't know he's autistic. And even if he is, it has nothing to do with luck. If there is any such thing as luck. Which I don't even believe in."

"How do you know?" said Mark. "Do you know what autism is? No. Nobody does. Autistic people can do amazing things."

"That's the stupidest thing I've ever heard," said John.

At this point Tony joined us. We all had to explain everything to him.

"Where is he now?" I asked.

"Who?" asked Mark.

"Joe."

"Probably at home. He never goes anywhere."

"Let's forget about golf for today and go get him," I said, looking at John.

"What are you thinking?" he said.

"We're all going for a little ride. Joe's driving."

John looked at me like I was an idiot. Like he was looking at someone who should know better. Superstitious, that's what he was thinking as he looked at me with disappointment. Joe was home, of course, and didn't seem to understand exactly why we were going out, but was happy to come. We drove for an hour and forty five minutes, all five of us. John didn't like doing it, but we forced him to. Resigned to what he thought was an exercise in silliness, he was determined to use it to put an end to the nonsense. He kept changing the route for Joe, trying to keep it totally random, in order to show us that there was nothing to it. And guess what happened?

Every traffic light was green.

Fifty of them.

How can I explain how weird that made me feel? John was incredulous. As we came home, he kept saying "I'll be damned. I'll be damned."

"We need to contact somebody," John said, after the drive was over. "This should be studied. This is a real phenomenon."

Mark was the first one to mention something about money.

"This is the luckiest guy I ever heard of. Why don't we get Joe to buy a Lotto ticket? We all sign an agreement, a contract that splits up the money. We get a lawyer to draw it up."

"I think I know somebody who would know how to get this studied by scientists," John said. "Most scientists wouldn't touch this, but there used to be some people at Duke University that studied this kind of thing."

"Why can't they study it after we're rich?" said Mark. "We don't want to tell anybody about this right now."

"Yeah," said Tony. "I like the idea about a contract."

"What are we going to do, each chip in twenty cents?" John sneered.

"That's right," I said. "We each chip in twenty cents in front of a witness. That makes us each legal owners of the ticket."

"Who's the witness? A lawyer?" said Mark. "Won't he want a cut too?"

But the lawyer didn't want a cut. He listened to us politely, but obviously thought we were a bunch of imbeciles. He agreed to write a contract, charging his usual hourly rate for an office visit. He was delighted to see us leave.

We let Joe buy the ticket. We elected one of us to hold it. It turned out to be Tony. The drawing was the next night, and I went through the two days trying not to let myself get too hopeful, but I couldn't stop it. I didn't sleep at all that night.

Money. A lot more of it than even we were used to. Except for Tony, who inherited his money and didn't have to work. But even he wasn't really rich. Was it actually possible? Could this really happen? Were we going to be rich?

By the time the drawing was held on TV, we were all wrecks. Nobody had slept much, and we looked pretty ragged. Tony had a brochure and had already picked out a yacht. When the first number came up on those little balls, none of us was breathing. And guess what happened?

We didn't get a single number right. It was a total bust. It was more than depressing, it was devastating. What had happened, we all wondered? We brainstormed it in the clubhouse the next day, but nobody could think of anything. Finally John asked if Joe had said or done anything unusual when the lights had all been green or the parking places had opened up, something he hadn't done when we bought the lotto ticket. I couldn't think of anything and said that all he talked about was the normal stuff everybody says.

"What exactly did he say? What is normal stuff?" said John.

At that point, the Four Doctors, as we called that perennial foursome, asked if we were going to tee off now. It was our tee time and we were starting to hold everybody up.

"He said he wished we didn't have to sit at red lights so much," I said, as we made our way to the first tee.

Everybody immediately looked at me.

"What?" asked John. "He said that exactly?"

Before I could answer, Mark chipped in.

"When we were going to the mall, he said he wished we didn't have to park so far away from the store every time. And that's when the parking space opened up right in front of the store. It happened again, too, a little later."

Mark and Tony were getting excited by this time. We were all standing in a group on the elevated first tee, which overlooked the clubhouse and the entrance to the subdivision.

"It's what he wishes for!" said Tony.

"He wished for that TV at Best Buy and didn't get it," I pointed out. "This has to do with something more complex than just wishing for things."

"Exactly," said John, nodding emphatically. "This is the twenty-first century. You people act like you're in the Dark Ages." He was looking at Tony and Mark. "I admit there is something odd here, but it isn't magic. We should contact somebody to study this. It's a statistical anomaly, maybe. A temporary perturbation of the normal rules of chance. This could be huge, mathematically speaking." He looked at me like he was confiding something to me that the others wouldn't understand.

"I don't know what that means," said Tony. "It won't get in the way of my getting my yacht, will it?"

Suddenly John froze, staring intently out at something on the road. I turned and immediately saw what it was.

"Look!" I said, pointing.

A truck was driving through the gate into our neighborhood. It was a Best Buy truck.

We all looked at each other.

"You don't think....?" I left the question unfinished.

We all left our cart and bags sitting at the tee and ran down through the shrubbery to the street. We followed the truck around the corner and watched it pull into Joe's driveway. It was a stunned group of us that stood there in the street as the delivery men took out the plasma TV and carried it into Joe's house. He had won the contest. It was the TV he had wished for.

"God almighty," said Tony. "Look at that, John. If this is an 'anomaly', I want in on the 'anomaly'."

"Yeah," said Mark. "I want some of that 'anomaly' too."

We all agreed, except for John. We decided we needed to know what Joe wished for, and jump on it quickly. John was contemptuous of our gullibility, but he was conflicted. I could see that even though he didn't believe in luck, he thought that if this was truly an anomaly, he might actually benefit from it. Finally, reluctantly, he joined in. We set up a schedule. Whenever Joe wished for something that we thought might make us rich, one of us, whoever was there with him at the time, would call the others. And we worked it out so one of us would be with him all of the time.

Two days later, Joe was in the car with me, and he said he wished the malls weren't so far away. He was looking at the field just across from our subdivision.

"Are you saying you want a mall close by here, Joe?" I asked.

"I wish there was a mall right there," he said, looking at that field.

I had been taking Joe and his son home, and as soon as they were out of the car, I called John on my cell phone.

"This is it," he said. "We need to buy that land immediately. I'll look into it right now. I'll call you back."

I was starting to get excited. It was only ten minutes until John phoned back.

"The land's for sale. There's no indication of anybody looking into it yet. Why don't you call all the others and see what they want to do. I've got the agent on the other line."

I contacted the others while I was driving. They were ecstatic. All of them said they were in. I relayed that to John.

"How do they want to handle this? How do I buy the land? Do they want me to buy it out of my account and have them pay me back? It's got to be a straight purchase. A loan would take time. Ask them and phone me back. I can do it right now."

I called and they all agreed. We were almost giddy. I told John we were all aboard and he signed a contract for the land. That evening, we all met John's lawyer, signed the papers, and paid back our share to John.

"What do we do now?" asked Tony.

"We wait," said John.

"How long?" asked Mark.

"I don't know," John admitted.

That put a damper on the exhilaration. I guess we all assumed we would get rich pretty much immediately. Slowly our lives got back to a semblance of dull normality. John had to go off on a business trip to Dallas. A depressing week went by without anything happening. Well, at least we had the land, we thought. It was an investment, if nothing else, but the initial ebullience had definitely worn off.

We discussed it endlessly. We started worrying that Joe didn't wish for the mall any more, so we got into the habit of asking him every day.

"You still want the mall, don't you, Joe?"

"Yes," he would always say. He never elaborated.

"You still want it in that field across from our subdivision, don't you?" we kept insisting, keeping him nudged in that direction.

"Yes," he would always say.

We were all getting antsy. Among us, we had put a lot of money into that land. Still nothing happened.

At the beginning of the next week, Joe's family called and said his sister was very sick and he needed to come home. It was like our little group was breaking up instead of getting rich.

Then, the first of the following week, John called me from Dallas. The agent had called him on his cell phone. He had asked if the land was for sale. He said he might have a potential buyer.

"Someone is definitely sniffing around," John exclaimed, letting a little of his fervor show in spite of himself. "I asked someone I know in the business, and he said he had heard a rumor, a big rumor about a new mall in our immediate area, but I couldn't get him to tell me what it was. Professional ethics. But I can read between the lines."

I called every one of our group. Our emotions skyrocketed. That evening, we had a little celebration party in my backyard. Those of us who were in town, anyway. It was too bad that Joe and John were both away. We talked about that. Nobody seemed to know when they were coming back. We were half drunk when my wife came out and said there were several policemen at the front door. Everybody looked at each other, wondering what this could mean. All of us all went out onto my front lawn and looked at the police car in my driveway. Two policemen stood there, along with a nerdy looking guy with disheveled hair and thick black glasses.

"Yes?" I said tentatively.

"We are here to inquire about the commission of a crime in this area…"

"We didn't know that using that autistic guy to get rich was a crime. We'll give it all back," blurted out Tony.

"Shut up," said Mark.

"What'd he say?" said the policemen, suddenly suspicious. He eyed all of us.

"Nothing," I said. "He has a medical condition."

The policeman looked sharply at Tony, and then continued. "There are two guys working as a team. Sometimes they bring in other people as accomplices. One is using a transmitter."

"Transmitter?" I said.

"Do you mean transmitters like the ones to open garage doors?" said Mark.

"Yes," said the policeman.

Everyone breathed a huge sigh of relief. The stress of having police at my door vanished. Everybody was suddenly cooperative.

"We all know that there is a danger of transmitters being used to open our garage doors. We all keep the doors from the garage to the house locked," said Tony.

"This is different," said the policeman.

The nerdy guy then started talking.

"The transmitters are used to cause an anomalous exiting from nominal sequencing of signal presentation for the purpose of determining the integrity of internal systems performance."

The others looked blankly at each other, but I didn't like the sound of it. The policeman stared at the nerdy guy with a look that said don't use those big words for these simple people.

"He talks like that all the time. He can't help himself. What he means is that the transmitters aren't used for garage doors. They are used for something else. They're Department of Transportation transmitters. Nobody else is supposed to have them. They're used to test equipment. This is what one looks like."

He showed us one.

"It looks like a garage door opener to me. What is it for, then?" said Mark.

"You point it at a traffic light at an intersection, and press the button here."

"Yeah?"

"And it forces the red light to turn green."

Beaner

By Buzz Bernard

Glad to be off Georgia 400 before the afternoon checkered flag dropped, turning the freeway into a static display of high-end automobiles; glad to be home early, Darren Nicholson turned his Lexus off Old Alabama Road into the Magnolia Heights Country Club subdivision.

On top of everything else, he was glad to be free of the moronic drivers who, like rats fleeing a scuttled ship, would scurry onto the roads in another couple of hours. Just once, he thought, it'd be nice to still have the clapped-out Chevy he'd driven in Boston, hurtling along Storrow Drive where the right of way went to the guy in the biggest, rustiest beater. Not to these dorks whipping their BMWs and Mercedes through north Fulton traffic like they were competing in an autocross.

He slowed as he entered the subdivision, relaxing as he glided beneath a verdant canopy of sweet gums, magnolias, and Bradford pears drooping over White Oak Drive. A jogger, bathed in a sheen of perspiration, waved at Darren. "Idiot," Darren mouthed. *Why not wait another hour before running? It'll be even hotter then.*

From White Oak, he turned right into Cherokee Lane and descended toward his house at the bottom of a cul-de-sac. But before he reached his driveway, something caught his eye at the side of the road. "Damn beaners." He stopped the car, got out, and approached a Hispanic yard worker. "Hey, Pancho, this yours?" He pointed at an empty Chik-fil-A carton in the gutter.

The worker shrugged.

"Well, Pancho, I don't give a good goddamn if it's yours or not. We pay you and your wetback buddies to keep this place clean. So how about makin' like Speedy Gonzales and pickin' it up."

"Sí, señor." The worker laid down the edger he'd been using and walked toward the curb.

"Ya know, maybe you guys would be better off chowin' down at Taco Bell instead of bringin' your lunch back here and leavin' trash all over."

"Sí, señor." The worker bent to pick up the carton. He had on an Atlanta Braves baseball cap, a sweat-stained tee-shirt, and raggedy jeans.

"You a big Braves fan, Pancho?"

"Sí, señor."

"Yeah, I'll bet you have box seats. Or do you just sneak into the games illegally?"

The worker nodded.

"Don't understand a word I'm sayin', do you, beaner? Okay, Pancho, beat feet. Chop, chop. Back to work." Darren shooed the man away with a dismissive flick of his hand.

The worker, probably in his late 20s with dark, penetrating eyes and a bushy mustache, tipped his hat. *"Día bueno, señor."* He crumpled the carton and stuffed it into the back pocket of his jeans. He turned and walked away.

Darren returned to his car, glad to be away from the stinking Mexican and out of the searing August heat. As he approached his house, he could see the garage door open and his wife, Tina, inside the garage folding up tables and chairs. She waved at him as he stopped the car and got out.

"What's up, honey?" he said. From somewhere in the neighborhood the distant yells and laughter of children, the purr of a lawnmower, the raspy call of a crow reached his ears. A chipmunk, its tail on Viagra, darted across the driveway.

"You're home early," she said.

"Never too early for a little afternoon delight." He tried to leer as he approached her.

She laughed. "Anyone in particular in mind?"

At forty, she was still a tease, still a good-looking woman. White shorts showcased her long, tan legs, and a clinging cotton blouse emphasized the gentle, glacial slope of her breasts. And even though her obsidian hair had turned prematurely salt-and-pepper, she still got hit upon regularly at the club. Apparently it didn't matter that everyone knew she was married. Or that they were playing with fire…he'd cold-cocked more than one jerk who'd had too many martinis and thought he was James frigging Bond.

"Hey, what are you doing out here?" he said, ignoring her question.

"Cleaning up."

"I mean with the chairs and everything."

She brushed a strand of hair out of her eyes, smiled at him. "I had some guests for lunch."

"In the garage?"

"The yard workers. They're always doing a little extra for us. I thought it'd be nice for them to sit down and enjoy a quiet meal. You know, some burgers, potato salad, baked beans."

He slammed the briefcase he'd been carrying onto the garage floor. "Honey, no, no, no." He strode toward her and grabbed her shoulders. "Look at me.

Promise me you'll never do this again. You don't know these guys, babe. Don't encourage them. Don't cater to them. They're criminals, gang bangers, dopers…"

She removed his hands from her shoulders and stepped back, her eyes firing invisible lasers. "What, like those yokels from the north Georgia mountains you hired to paint our living room?"

"Okay. A bad call. But they were cheap."

"They were meth heads. The room ended up looking like a paint sampler at Sherwin-Williams."

"They didn't get paid."

"Yeah, they were real happy about that." She tipped a table on its side. "Help me with this," she said. "Look, at least you get an honest day's work from the Hispanics."

"There's nothing honest about them. They're illegals." He folded the metal legs of the table and snapped them flush against the underside.

"They may or may not be. You don't know. All I know is they're hard workers. They contribute to the economy, pay taxes and take jobs nobody else will." She nodded toward his golf bag at the back of the garage. "Thanks to the 'illegals,' as you call them, you can go out every weekend and whack your little golf ball around instead of whacking weeds. Put the table over there." She pointed to where she wanted it.

"Hard workers. Bullshit. Look at the DUI stops and drug busts listed in the paper every week. Half of them are greasers. They piss in our streets. Drive uninsured. Use our emergency rooms like free clinics. Guess who foots the bill for all that?" He slammed the table into a corner of the garage. "I want you to stay away from them. You don't think, given half an opportunity, these guys wouldn't like to knock off a nice little piece of North American tail?"

"Last time I looked, Mexico *was* part of North America," she snapped. She whirled and stalked toward the house. "But don't worry, they aren't going to get a little piece of tail, as you so delicately put it. Nor is someone else I know, Mr. Sensitivity." She flounced into the house and shut the door in his face.

He stood, hands on hips, staring at the closed door. "Goddamn beaners," he muttered. He kicked a trashcan standing near the front of the garage. It toppled over, spilling its putrid contents of soiled paper plates, dripping plastic cups, and empty aluminum cans into the driveway. One of the cans tumbled end over end to the bottom of the drive as two yard workers, one of them the man Darren had chastised moments ago, walked past.

The man stopped, looked at Darren, then bent to pick up the can.

"Just leave it, Pancho," Darren shouted. "Just frigging leave it."

*　　*　　*　　*

Black and white cauliflowers of clouds, signatures of a departing summer storm, billowed above the northeast horizon. Distant thunder grumbled, then faded away on a humid breeze. Spirals of steam rose from the damp road leading to Darren's house as the late-afternoon sun burned away pools of rainwater left by the storm.

Good enough, Darren thought as he drove toward his house. It'll be dry in half an hour and there'll still be enough daylight left for me to get in nine holes. He pulled around a battered Ford Fiesta bearing dealer plates parked at the curb. "Jesus," he muttered, "now we've become a parking lot for Tijuana taxis." He reached for the remote-control garage door opener on the underside of the rearview mirror. But he didn't press the button. The door already was open. He pulled in beside Tina's car. The door leading from the garage to the house was open too. He surmised Tina must be carting some groceries from her car into the pantry.

He retrieved his briefcase, stepped from the car and glanced behind Tina's. No wet tire tracks. Her car, then, had been in the garage for quite some time. Not like Tina to leave the door to the house ajar on a hot, humid afternoon. He walked to the doorway and looked down. His stomach knotted. Muddy footprints smudged the entryway tile. Not dainty prints. Large prints. Workman's boots. "Honey?" he called. No answer. His heart rate accelerated and he found himself suddenly struggling for oxygen, his breath coming in short, airless gasps. "Tina," he called again, louder. Silence. He sensed someone behind him, whirled.

It was the beaner he'd had the run-in with. The man stood, hat in one hand, pointing toward the door with the other. *"Gran problema,"* he said, *"hombres malos."*

"Problema, Pancho? What the hell are you babbling about?" Darren stepped toward the man.

The yard worker's eyes darted from Darren to the interior. He stepped back. *"Hombres malos,* he repeated. *"Su esposa—"*

"English, pepper belly," Darren demanded. His anger rose. This guy was up to something. He was scared, nervous.

"Su esposa, señor. Your wife. I try to find my *amigo* to help—"

"My wife? My wife? You and your Mexican bud after my wife?" Adrenaline took over. His anger surged out of control. He whipped his briefcase up in a swift, violent motion, catching the Hispanic underneath his chin. The man's head snapped back, blood spraying from his mouth. He crumpled to the garage floor, a straw man caught in a thunderstorm downburst. Darren bent over him. "I'll show you what a problema is, Pancho. Don't ever come near my wife, my home, or me again."

The man moaned.

Darren stood, delivered a sharp kick to the beaner's stomach. The moaning ceased.

Darren stepped into the entryway, stopped, and listened. He thought he heard something, a whimper or soft cry perhaps, from the far end of the house, toward the master bedroom. But he couldn't be sure over the constant hum of the air conditioner.

He slipped off his shoes, not wanting to give Pancho's accomplice any more warning than he'd already had, and eased into the kitchen. The odor of barbecued spareribs and potato salad, Tina's dinner preparations, filled the room. He withdrew a carving knife from the butcher's block. Then, staying close to the walls, knife at the ready, he edged silently through the dining and family rooms into the hallway leading to the master bedroom. He crept past the study and a guest bedroom and reached the entrance to the master.

He stopped, remaining just out of sight of anyone who might be in the bedroom. He could hear his wife's voice now, though it was muffled and indistinct. What was clear, however, was the terror that permeated it.

With his back to the wall, he leaned his head into the bedroom. What he saw triggered volcanic fury. His wife, face down on the bed, was gagged and bound. Her shorts and panties, shredded, draped over her ankles. A man, his back to Darren and a nylon stocking pulled over his head, straddled her naked bottom as he fumbled at the zipper of his pants.

Without a word, Darren stepped into the bedroom and raised the knife. He'd gone only two steps when he heard the distinctive sound of a round being chambered into an automatic. Cool metal pressed against the back of his neck.

"You gotta know when to hold 'em, know when to fold 'em, dick head. Nine millimeter beats a kitchen knife. Drop it." A voice from behind him. Not Hispanic.

The man astride Tina turned. He smiled. Through the nylon stocking his face took on the appearance of a leering, asymmetrical jack-o'-lantern.

"Drop it now or you're dead," the voice behind Darren commanded.

He dropped the knife. It thudded softly into the thick pile of the carpet. He saw Tina try to swivel her head and look back.

"We'll take turns," the voice said. "First, well, let's just call him Al, then me. You can be the judge, dude. Decide who does it better."

Darren knew the voice. He'd heard it before. Recently. It bore the twangy drawl of the Appalachian Mountains. He willed himself to focus, to think of a way out of this. To find the right words, calculate the right moves. He had to do something quickly. But he was in a dire situation and knew it. He swallowed twice, attempting to slow his spastic breathing before speaking. "Look," he said, after steadying himself, "let's just settle up for the painting you did. Double the going rate. You don't need to do this." He heard his wife whimper, saw the fear in her eyes.

"What are you talking about, man? We never been here before. Let's see if I can figure this out. Sounds like maybe you didn't ante up for some work you had done. And now you think we're the guys, like taking it out in trade or something. Naw, we're just a couple a good ole country boys lookin' for some big city fun."

"I think you'd better renounce your membership in Mensa, asshole. I know who the hell you are."

"Renounce my what?"

"I'll give you a chance to redeem yourself, hillbilly. Four thousand bucks. Four times what you were gonna earn." The man didn't respond immediately. Maybe I've reached him, Darren thought.

"Well, a shit lotta good money's gonna do us if you think you got us pegged."

"You leave here with the money, I don't call the cops."

"Oh, don't worry, you ain't gonna call the cops, you country club prick."

Darren realized he hadn't reached the guy. Only managed to harden his position. He heard a small cry from Tina. The guy kneeling on top of her had worked his zipper down.

He lowered himself onto her buttocks. She thrashed and squirmed violently, but her actions earned her only a powerful slap on the side of her head. Then a second one. Darren lurched toward the man, but was spun around sharply by an arm thrust across his throat from behind. He found himself staring directly into the barrel of the automatic.

Even through the nylon stocking pulled tight over the gunman's face he could see dilated eyes dancing on meth. Eyes that reflected no morality, no compassion. Eyes that suggested a conscience unable to discriminate between robbery and rape, or rape and murder. All of equal weight. All of no weight.

Darren calculated the odds. Piss poor, he judged. He'd heard of guys being missed by bullets fired at point blank range, but wasn't sure the tales were true. Still, maybe with a guy strung out on meth.... He had to try. He and his wife were probably going to be murdered anyhow. He tensed his muscles, ready to launch his forearm upward in an attempt to knock the 9mm away before the man could pull the trigger. Too late. The gunman smashed the barrel of the weapon into his face.

Darren reeled backward, sprawling onto the carpet, the room spinning.

"Dumb idea, jerk off. I'm not brain dead, just high. I don't really wanna mess up the bedroom before I get my rocks off."

For all the world, it sounded like an aluminum bat slamming into a ripe cantaloupe. The gun tumbled from the man's hand and he staggered forward, then back, then forward again before performing a pirouette and collapsing beside Darren.

Darren attempted to focus, see what was happening. He saw a figure moving toward his wife, toward her assailant. The figure carried something long and slender in his hands, drew it back like a batter ready to hit a baseball. The assailant turned, raised his hands in a protective gesture. The figure swung whatever he carried. A whistling sound filled the room, a swoosh like a driver knifing toward a golf ball on a tee. Tina's assailant screamed an obscenity, toppled off her sideways onto the floor. Tina screamed, too, rolled from the bed. The figure swung again, lashing his makeshift weapon directly down from above onto the seemingly stunned assailant.

Darren's vision cleared slightly. He saw something separate from the end of the weapon and fly into the air after smashing the intruder's face. Darren grabbed the 9mm that lay on the floor beside him and crawled toward his wife who huddled next to the bed. He pulled a sheet from the bed to cover her. "It's okay, baby," he said, "it's okay. The bad guys are down." He peeked over the top of the bed. Blood dribbled into his throat, forcing him to swallow before speaking. "Hey, Pancho," he called, *"gracias."*

The Hispanic yard worker tossed the broken shaft of Darren's TaylorMade R7 driver onto the floor and walked out.

* * * *

The Roswell police had finished their business, the EMTs had departed, the crowd of neighbors had dispersed and the last of the local television reporters had wrapped up their interviews. Darren and Tina stood with their rescuer on the front porch of their home. The evening had turned soft—pink and gold—and an easy breeze rustled the leaves of the sweet gums surrounding the house. A chorus of night peepers began to sing, pianissimo at first, then forte.

Darren handed the Hispanic man his business card. "I can get you a job at my company," he said. "My way of saying thanks. My way of apologizing."

The Hispanic rubbed his heavily bandaged chin. "I'm an illegal," he said.

"We can get around that."

The Hispanic smiled. "No thank you, *señor*. I think I will be better off staying where I am. With a man who treats me with respect, who calls me Eduardo, my real name, not Pancho, and knows I am Honduran, not Mexican. And I think, even though you may be an important person at…" He lifted the business card closer to the porch light so he could read it. "…Golden Pyramid Corporation, you could learn a lot about being good to people from your wife." He nodded in Tina's direction.

Tina slapped at a mosquito on her arm, then punched her husband softly on his shoulder.

"You suddenly speak very good English…Eduardo," Darren said.

"I always have, *señor*. I was a good student. But sometimes when I get angry or excited it is Spanish that comes out."

Darren extended his hand for Eduardo to shake. "I was out of line in the garage this afternoon. And last week when we first met. I apologize for that. Thanks again for being man enough to overlook my actions and help us. At your peril, I might add."

Eduardo accepted the proffered hand. "People here judge us too much by our accent and our skin color, I think. They don't get to know us as Juan or Pedro, like your wife did. We are not all Speedy in a sombrero. *Buenos noches, señor.* Take good care of your wife. She is a good woman."

"I know."

Eduardo walked down the steps toward a waiting car.

"Eduardo," Darren said.

The Honduran turned.

"What kind of beer do you like?"

"Michelob."

"Next Friday night I'd like you and your friends to come over. We'll grill steaks and drink Michelob."

Eduardo smiled. "Okay."

"And, Eduardo?"

"*Sí, señor?*"

"Bring some pictures of your family."

How to Live When You're Away From Me

By Terry Segal

Don't be careless with my life that you live. Wear light colors after dark. Don't run with scissors or a lollipop in your mouth. Balloons are the number-one choking hazard for children under the age of five. If you're hiking, whatever you do, don't put a plastic bag on your head. Don't talk while you're chewing, you might choke. Put the stick down, you could take someone's eye out with that. If the lodge is too cold, never put a space heater in your bath water.

Don't drink and drive. Don't drink and talk to loose women. Don't drink at all. Don't jump up and down after you eat, you could throw up. In case you should suddenly decide to wear them, buy flame-resistant, not just flame-retardant, pajamas. Don't step on a crack; your mother has enough going on. Don't take the tags off pillows. Hold the blade away from you while cutting your bagel. If you get caught in an undertow, remember to swim parallel to the shore. Moss grows on the north side of the trees and make sure the trail back to my heart is clear. Don't leave breadcrumbs. Birds eat them. Never barbeque your Christmas tree to get rid of it—with or without the tinsel. Brush your teeth before you go to bed. Don't say anything you wouldn't want printed on the front page of the newspaper. Say your prayers. I'll be saying mine.

Don't tax your guardian angels. Look behind the door for instructions, even if you won't read them. Bring your seat-back to an upright position with the tray table securely fastened. Keep your eyes on the road, both hands on the wheel. Buckle your seat belt. Carry traveler's checks. Don't talk to strangers or take any wooden nickels.

If you have a splinter, paint it with rubber cement and when it dries, peel it off. For boo-boos, blow on them, and then kiss them. Don't play with matches or snakes. Don't try to keep your eyes open when you sneeze. Bundle up. Snuggle in and know that I love you.

Red in the Post Office

By Cecilia Branhut

The temptation to boast about her offspring was so strong that the Woman in Red had given in to it—totally, loudly, stridently.

She was at the head of the line in the post office, and as I entered, a woman directly in front of me looked at me appealingly, as if I had arrived at just the right moment and would save them all from this onslaught.

The words were being delivered to an acquaintance, the Woman in Grey. She was so grey that she was virtually invisible next to the red. And that's how she wanted it. She gave answers, but they were soundless, even in the hushed post office. Clearly, she ached to disappear, but there was no escape.

On and on went the Woman in Red. Apparently, the people behind the counter were sadists; all they had to do was say, "Next," but they seemed to slow down deliberately. It was obviously never going to be her turn.

Finally, I realized all the other customers were looking around, pleading with their eyes for someone to rescue them. I had to do it.

I marched to the head of the line until I was eyeball-to-eyeball with the Woman in Red. She totally misunderstood my intention. I felt revulsion and anger; she saw admiration and interest. I knew that trying to outdo her in volume was useless. I remembered that talking softly and calmly is always the most effective way to get one's point across. I began to speak slowly and quietly. She was looking at me directly and must have seen my mouth moving. But she didn't miss a beat. On and on she went, layering boast upon boast. I raised my purse menacingly, about to take the only course open to me. I was going to hit her, hit her, hit her, and no one was going to stop me.

"Next!"

It was her turn and it was over.

The Bargain King

By Walter Lawrence

People said my father was cheap. No, actually they said he was The Bargain King.

Maybe. It's true enough that he was careful with his money. And, I know for an undisputed fact that he really loved a good bargain. It was no secret that my dad would go out of his way to find a deal, wherever it hid itself north of the Chattahoochee during those quiet days of the late 1960s.

Sometimes he would spend hours at a time in the most out of the way places trying to track down his next unlikely find. I know that, too, from experience. Dad would drag me along with him most of the time, as though it were some rite of passage that would bond together the male members of our tribe.

But, in the end, he might have saved only two dollars on an item that might have started out at fifteen. Take, for example, the time we came home with a pickup truckload of 2"x4" lumber. I'd never seen my dad use a hammer or saw a day in his life. But he loved those boards.

Here was the fun part. Dad said the two dollars he saved went into *the kitty*. I never did figure out where that kitty was kept, although I looked for it hard enough. Eventually, I concluded that the kitty was some mythical scoreboard Dad kept in the back of his head. Only my father knew whether he was ahead or behind after all those years of hunting. (Later he sold that lumber to a friend for a twenty-dollar profit. We went to lunch that weekend downtown at the Alpha Soda on Main Street; in Dad's mind, the meal was *free*.)

My father's friends and colleagues became befuddled when this discount-barn behavior continued after his business took off along with the growth of North Fulton, in that sleepy little part of the county that used to be Milton before the Depression bankrupted it. It was about that time I started high school. Dad had more money than he had ever seen in his life. But he continued to bargain hunt, and it seemed to his friends that he did it then with an increased enthusiasm and zeal. I believed that was true enough, because I could see that this was a big game to him now. Dad was good at it and he loved to play.

When I was a sophomore, a telling event happened to the Bargain King. His good friend and personal attorney, Jay Sam Levey, referred a new client to him. My father was a veterinarian. He was an exceptional surgeon on small animals. His professional claim to fame, however, was his stubborn effort, along with the help of two vets from nearby Cherokee County, to eradicate rabies in that part of North Georgia.

Jay Sam was a colorful individual who took pride in having some offbeat people among his well-heeled clientele. One of these unusual people was Herbert Talbot. Herbert stood only five-feet-seven in his very thick-soled shoes. In addition, he was built like a soft pear because his job required him to sit a lot—and drink beer and hard liquors in large quantities. Herbert was a professional gambler. He played poker mostly, but for big money. And, like most of his fellow gamblers, Herbert enjoyed his success in waves of feast or famine. Aside from cards and stout drinking, Herbert had two other mainstays in his life: a beautiful longhaired Irish setter named Muldoon, and a lovely fiancée who, it seemed to me, was quite young for a man of his advanced years.

On the day that Herbert was introduced to Dad, Muldoon had *violated Newton's Law*. That would be the one about "two objects could not occupy the same space at the same time." VNL was a phrase my father had coined to describe the medical condition succinctly. A car had hit Muldoon, and the dog was badly injured. Upon seeing Muldoon's condition, my dad told Herbert that putting the dog down was not out of the question. Dad said he could, of course, try to save Muldoon, but it would be very tricky. (The middle-aged gambler did not read into that, *expensive*.) Herbert was all sobs and blubbering, but his young fiancée looked altogether disinterested. I don't think she liked the dog much. Finally, Herbert Talbot insisted that Dad must try to save Muldoon. The dog, after all, had always been loyal and friendly. Besides that, Herbert sincerely believed his luck had changed for the better the day he bought the cherished red setter.

It was a long afternoon and night in surgery. I assisted my father and his helpers with that operation. Eventually, Dad was satisfied that the dog had been given the best chance to recover. Following that, Muldoon lived in the clinic for the next ten days or so with tubes stuck in his veins and dressings being changed around the clock, most often by my father himself. It seemed my dad had taken a liking to the wounded critter during the delicate healing process. The day finally came when the dog stood up on his own efforts and was able to stay there. Muldoon was declared, guardedly, fit enough to convalesce at home.

This is where the Cheap part comes in. It seems that, indeed, the dog had been Herbert's lucky charm. Being banged up like he was kept Muldoon from contributing to Herbert's good providence with cards. Herbert had hit a major dry spell. In fact, Jay Sam was forced to help the gambler out of some minor legal jams. So when it came time to pay the tab on Muldoon's surgery—which, as I said, was not inexpensive considering all that my father had to do to save the dog—Herbert had no money. But Dad was not upset too much. After all, he had known that Herbert was a gambler when this all started.

Dad just asked the man what kind of arrangements he could make to settle up. While Dad was discussing things with Herbert, I was looking closely at the dead-beat gambler, but more so at his young lady friend. She looked quite impatient, much like a society matron who was an hour late for the beauty parlor. The streak of bad luck seemed to be wearing on her more than on Herbert. She did not hear Herbert's suggestion the first time he made it. But she did feel it when he took her left hand and deftly slid the diamond ring off her finger. Herbert assured Dad that it was real. "How 'bout this, doc? A carat-and-a-half, will that settle it?"

My father's eyes looked like a man who just rubbed a banged-up old lamp and discovered the genie inside it. Obviously it was enough, probably more than enough. *And the IRS would never know.* When Herbert and the now-quarrelsome woman had left with Muldoon, Dad showed me the ring. It was big and angular. He called it an emerald cut. The stone was set in a thin platinum band.

The first thing I wondered was which one of his acquaintances would buy the ring. There had to be more than a deluxe hamburger plate in this one, maybe we'd even go to Lickskillet Farm over in Roswell. But my dad surprised me, and probably himself. "You know, son, I've never given your mother a diamond. We should probably see if she wants it."

My dad had now entered new territory, behavior-wise. And that led to a big logistical problem for him. In the first place, no one, especially my mother, was going to believe that my father would ever actually *pay* for a real diamond like that. So there was no way he was going to sell that version of the ring's acquisition. *Plan A.*

That left his fabled bargains. Dad knew that when he showed the ring to Mom, she would see it as the latest prize in his hunt for little treasures. She would undoubtedly believe that he paid something like two-cents-on-the-dollar for it, and that it was probably a fake. He would not generate much esteem from her with that line of thinking. *Plan B.*

What a dilemma: to be seen as either a liar or an incurable tightwad with no real notion of romance. What was the Bargain King to do? I watched him mull this over for a full ten minutes before we headed home that Saturday afternoon. I can report to you that the man did not get through vet school without having at least a little bit of brains. He went to *Plan C.*

The whole thing would have made no sense if I had not remembered that my dad was the man who once—wearing only an undershirt and striped boxer shorts—did a spirited rendition of the ballet *Swan Lake* after Mom forced him to sit through a traveling production of it at Agnes Scott College. He cavorted wildly throughout the den and dining room, jumping and turning in circles. And, this was the same man who sat night after night with me on one arm of his favorite chair and my sister on the other, reading to us from his favorite books of prose or poetry when we were younger. The big man was a softy and a romantic after all. You just tended to forget that about him.

Upon arriving home, he sat my mother down at the kitchen table, saying, "The man who owned Muldoon didn't have any money. He gave me this instead." Dad pulled the ring out of his pocket and dropped it into her palm. "I think it's much too beautiful to sell. Will you accept it as the diamond I promised to get you one day?" Total honesty with a little tug at the heartstrings, who would have thought that would have worked? My mother's response was all hugs and tears. The next thing I knew, my sister and I were being dropped off at my aunt's house for the night.

My mother lived to be seventy-six, long outlasting my father. She wore that ring and the matching wedding band he eventually bought her until shortly before she died. And, I'm happy to say that the woman I asked to marry me is equally happy to wear it now, too—gambling story, Muldoon, and all.

Sometimes when I see the diamond on my wife's finger, I cannot help but think of its legacy from the Bargain King.

Chocolate Deception

By Brooks Dumas

Lila licked warm, rich chocolate from her fingers. Sinful pleasure washed over her. This new recipe from the Roswell Methodist Ladies Auxiliary Cookbook for Chocolate Deception Bundt Cake was a love offering, rife with surprise bursts of plump, succulent cherries. Drizzling, sugary, chocolate glaze overflowed the center hole and ran sensuously down the sides of the cake into the channel ringing the cake platter. Chocolate. Her addiction. She fought the temptation to stuff huge, spongy chunks into her mouth. Just a lick would have to do. Just a slither of her tongue on the spatula. Bearing two children had widened her hips, but her passion for sweets had added pads of fat to her once slender figure. It wasn't fair. Her husband's physique was still firm and taut. He could devour two or three large helpings of cake without adding an ounce of fat to his heavenly body.

The door slammed. Donnie, Jr., whirled through the kitchen leaving a trail of Chattahoochee River mud on the newly mopped floor. A cane pole sprouted from one of his grimy little hands and a white bait carton marked Al's Roswell Bait and Tackle sprouted from the other.

"Mom, your left rear's on high."

Left rear? The stove. She wanted to shout, "Don't leave your fishing things in the kitchen," but he had vanished through the garage door in the instant it had taken her to flick off the hot eye of the stove. Lila leaned against the kitchen counter, daydreaming. Little boys seemed so innocent, so captivated with dirt and worms and boy things. It was hard to imagine boyhood innocence evolving into the lust of manhood. Would her son be like his father? Would he, too, hold his wife in the prison of his arms? As if her thoughts had conjured her husband to the kitchen, she felt rough hands slide up her back and inch around her sides to cup her breasts.

"Mmmm, chocolate cake. You really know how to take care of me."

Don licked the contour of her ear, and Lila was lost, lost in sensations that weakened her knees and sent warm tingles through her body. She twisted in his arms and poked a bite-sized morsel of cake into his mouth. He closed his eyes. His expression softened with the dreamy contentment Lila had seen so often in the aftermath of their lovemaking. At this moment his satisfaction was her fulfillment.

But something was wrong. His mouth had frozen in mid-chew. *An eggshell?*

His eyes flashed open, and he glared down at her. "What's this? Have you been experimenting again?" He pulled a chunk of cherry from his mouth and examined it distastefully. "Don't you get it? Can't you understand anything? I wanted a chocolate cake. No cherries. Chocolate. Is that so difficult?" He pushed her away from him. "What's this all over the floor? Let me guess.... Your son was here. Mud. Fishing gear in the kitchen. He's just like you. Never does anything right."

*   *   *   *

Lila poked fork holes in the chocolate sheet cake, allowing the glaze to seep into the cake's interior. She had gotten the message. No cherries *this* time. Maybe this would keep him home tonight. Maybe he'd even sleep with her. Sleep. She could use a nap. Waiting up last night had been torture. She hoped Don had been at his mother's house in Alpharetta, but she was probably kidding herself. She couldn't think about where he was last night. She didn't have time.

The grandfather clock bonged. Five o'clock. She still had to straighten the kitchen and scrub the floor before Don came home. She would remove all traces of D.J.'s latest fishing expedition. If she couldn't make Don love his little son, she could at least try to avert his anger.

*   *   *   *

"Wrong again! I asked you to make a cake just like the last one, only no cherries. I wanted a round cake with a hole in the middle, with icing filling up the hole and running down the sides. This cake is rectangular. At least you got one thing right. It *is* chocolate. Have you forgotten what my mother told you? A good Southern wife cooks exactly what her husband wants, with that secret ingredient, Tender Loving Care. Not cherries. I hate rectangular cakes." He dumped the cake, pan and all, into the trash. Hot tears spilled down Lila's cheeks. She licked the salty residue from the corners of her mouth. "I have no intention of staying to watch you blubber like a baby. I'm outta here. And don't call my mother. She won't tell you anything."

Lila's stomach ached with the pain of rejection. Her tender feelings stung with the lash of Don's words. She had failed again. *The cake should have been round? Shape is important? I guess I didn't think. Don would say that's exactly my problem. I never think. I don't seem to have the power to please him. For that matter, I don't seem to have any power left at all. Maybe if I just disappeared, we'd both be happy. But there's D.J. to think of. He needs a home, a father. Who am I kidding? I should be honest with myself. I've become really good at making excuses. I'm addicted to Don just like I'm addicted to that chocolate cake.*

Dejectedly, she began to straighten the kitchen. She took D. J.'s mud-caked shoes into the laundry room. The fishing pole would have to go in the garage. Lila shook the bait carton and opened it to see if anything was still alive. Inside, masses of wigglers writhed around each other, tunneling through the dark, loamy soil. A few, desperate for different surroundings, stretched their tentacle bodies toward the mouth of the container. Mesmerized, she envisioned herself in the container with the worms, struggling to exist. In that instant she knew it was all a matter of choice. Lila shuddered and quickly closed the lid, wondering how many of God's creatures sought escape from meaningless lives of quiet desperation.

*   *   *   *

"Now that's chocolate cake! You finally got it right. Round, with a hole in the middle, and icing running out of the hole down the sides."

Lila buried her face in Don's chest to hide her expression. He wrapped her lovingly in the circle of one arm and devoured a generous piece of cake. "Want a bite?" He held the confection to her lip. Her stomach rose in her throat. Suppressing the urge to gag, she clenched her teeth and turned her head away. "One little bite won't hurt. Hey, why don't I take Mother a piece of this cake right now? She'll be so pleased with you." He lifted her chin with the tip of his forefinger. "I can see from the look on your face you're pretty pleased with yourself." Don kissed her forehead and left, proudly taking the cake with him.

Lila turned back to the sink. She scrubbed and soaked and scalded the blender three more times, wondering if she would ever be able to use it again. And what would she tell D. J. when he asked what she had done with his bait?

The Mammogram

By Terry Segal

We all sat in the crowded room at Northside Hospital Women's Center in Atlanta, and waited for our results. The banker, the doctor, the educator, most of us mothers as well—grandmothers and homemakers waited. We had all received the same letter; the one whose words blurred after that first horrifying sentence next to the box with the checkmark that read, "Further diagnostic mammogram required."

"Never let 'em see you sweat," the slogan says, yet there we were, stripped of our deodorants, antiperspirants, blouses, bras, body creams and powders, as we had been instructed. Also taken from us were our public faces that usually exude strength and serenity. We had to check our Superwoman capes and tights at the door and don the white, linen robes. I pretended I was at the spa until we were told to sit in chairs. I stood at first, refusing to let others dictate my actions, but a heat weakened my knees and I slid on to the vinyl seat of the chair on the end.

A video played on the elevated TV in the corner. It was politically correct as it portrayed women of every color giving themselves breast exams. Its message was haunting. *Neither race, nor religion, nor fashion-sense exempts you. You could have breast cancer.* No one watched. What good was it? If they really cared, they'd have sent those women to our homes to check our breasts and it would've been well before we had each received that letter.

The silence was shattered when the heavy door opened. The Voice called someone's name. An android woman among us rose and disappeared through the door. We heard her footsteps echo down the hall. We sat motionless, barely breathing and avoiding eye contact.

Why hadn't I read the statistics more thoroughly? I always sponsor walkers in the 3-Day Walk for the Cure. Was it one-in-six women who walk through that door and get sent down another hallway? I occupied myself with counting the number of women in the room in an attempt to figure out my odds.

Suddenly, I was in Sartre's play, *No Exit*. It's about people who wait in a room to learn whether they will go to heaven or hell. It turns out that waiting in the room *is* hell.

I breathed deeply, both in and out. I had not done that for twenty minutes or so. Maybe I had never done it. The android woman returned. Surely they had not mistakenly x-rayed her mouth. Her lips were flat and compressed. She leaned over me to use the phone on the end table, but refused to let me get up and give her my seat. Does my chair have a black mark underneath it and she doesn't want to sit in it? Her breasts, beneath the thin gown, hung loosely near my face. Why won't she let me get up? I wondered.

Being a seasoned psychotherapist, I was able to recognize that, inside of my head, I sounded like a crazy person. Then paranoia set in. It occurred to me that that's how androids are created. Fear paralyzes the personality and the physical body moves to outer directed commands. Well, they wouldn't get me.

"It is," the woman on the phone whispered to someone she probably loved and who loved her in return.

"It is…*what*?" I wanted to shriek. "*What*?" It is *cancer*? It is *clear*? *What*? Was she the one-in-six or was she using code so that we wouldn't know she'd passed that card to another one of us?

"Miss Segal?" The Voice called. I had filled out the form. Didn't she read it? The choices had read, "Mrs., Miss, Ms., and Dr." I proudly had checked "Dr.," having worked so hard to achieve my Ph.D. More often than not here, people assume that Dr. Segal is my husband. The forms for women never used to include a box marked "Dr." Even though I had checked that one, I'd now been stripped of that too. I didn't look at the others and just walked through the door.

Once on the other side, The Voice spoke to me. I was happy to see she also had a face—a gentle, open face. A face that had chosen her profession because she loves people and wants to help, I decided. There had just been too many of us for her to read that box I checked. It was much more important that she read the x-rays correctly.

I stepped up to the archaic mammogram device of torture. The Voice with the Face contorted me, and pressed my ribs against the plate until they ached. She trapped my right breast and imprisoned it in the glass sliding doors, trying to capture the best angle of its innermost privacy. She instructed me to hold my breath. No problem doing that. I had to remind myself to breathe at all.

I was sent back to the waiting room to wait. That is what you do in a waiting room; wait, among other things. You also search your soul to determine what you're made of. Or you mindlessly flip through magazines with photos of bleached-teeth beauties to avoid that. I returned to my seat on the end, *my* seat, as though it had been assigned. I leapt up, just in case there was a black mark and decided to stand.

Pacing, I called my husband on my cell phone. I didn't want to use that other phone. Maybe that was a bad news phone and I didn't want to touch it. The android woman was gone. I sent a prayer along after her and decided to send prayers to everyone in there.

"SHOULDN'T WE BE TALKING ABOUT THIS?" I shrieked inside of my head, again. "SHOULDN'T WE BE TALKING ABOUT HOW SCARED WE ARE?" Maybe we should just be bargaining with God. Maybe just I should. Why do I always feel as though I need to take care of everyone else? Maybe I could bargain with God like I did when I was younger. I would pray to get my period and promise to be more careful and more responsible next time. This had to be in the same department, under Female Issues.

My husband answered the phone.

I had bravely told him and my oldest daughter that I didn't need company on this trip because they wouldn't let them in the room where it counted, anyway. I had passed through the outer waiting room of men. There were loving, supportive men of all ages, mindlessly flipping through financial report magazines, trying to avoid an exploration of their souls that might make them whisper aloud that they were scared. I felt sorry for them. Helpless sideline coaches, they were. Some would unexpectedly be called in to coach the big game, without any prior experience.

"Hi. I'm waiting for the results," I told my husband. "That's what you do in a waiting room. You wait." I began to cry. My lip quivered like it did when I was eight years old and had fallen off my bike. I'd seen the blood on my knee and thought I'd bleed to death before I could make it the two blocks to my home. I tried to be brave.

As I spoke to him, I noticed the sign that instructed us to quit sniveling and go into the black void alone. It actually read, "The use of cell phones is prohibited." I knew what it really meant. He and I spoke briefly, as I pressed myself into a locker for privacy that I didn't have. I promised to call him back after I had spoken again to The Voice with the Face.

Not usually a rule breaker, I'd also refused to use the locker they gave me. Instead, I had stuffed my clothes into my shoulder bag in case I decided to flee. Racking sobs forced their way into my throat, carrying enough tears for everyone in the room. I choked them back, however, because I'd read the manual on appropriate waiting room decorum.

A dark, brown hand appeared on the shoulder of my white, linen gown.

I turned my head and looked into the face of the dark-skinned angel, poised to receive the message she had for me.

"Don't cry," she said softly, which only released my deluge of tears. "You are not alone."

No kidding! I was in a room with twenty other people. Oh, I realized she meant God.

"Just pray," she said. "Release your fear." She told me that God had told her, "Everything is fine." She said to me, "You are fine. Even if you get the news you don't want to hear, God is present and He will help you through it."

I wrapped my arms around her, aware that our breasts hugged each other through our gowns, and thanked her. I wondered if anyone else saw her in the room. Maybe they just saw the wild-eyed woman who screams in her head, hugging the air by the lockers that she refused to use. I was long overdue for another breath.

"Miss Segal?" Ugh! Again. Okay. Not important.

I had wanted to explain to the angel that it's *my* job to comfort people, *my* job to remind them that they are not alone and that "bidden or not bidden, God is always present." I felt guilty that I hadn't done that for her. Then I remembered that someone told me we rob others of feeling good when we don't let them help us when we need it. I had needed it *big time*. She had been there and I was grateful. God had already been there for her ahead of me so she was fine. And she was. The one-in-six was still among us.

Hadn't those other women moved from their seats? The Voice motioned for me to follow her into the hallway again. If I were also fine, why wouldn't she just blurt that out and let me leave? She stopped, just behind the door, and looked at me as if she held a secret to my future. If I were not fine, how cold would it be to tell me right there? Why wouldn't she take me in a room, wrap me in a cozy blanket and give me milk and cookies?

"You are fine," she said, echoing the black angel's words.

I *know*! I wanted to scream again. *She* just told me and God told *her*, but what does the mammogram show?

"It is just a cyst," The Voice with the Face said. "We knew that it was, but it had changed. Sometimes they do. We'll see you for your exam next year. You are free to leave."

"I am cancer-free to leave," I heard.

I wept with relief. I didn't look at the other women as I left because I didn't want them to know that I handed them the one-in-six card that wasn't mine. I flooded the room with prayer and slipped into a restroom. I yanked clothes from the bag and threw them on as I fumbled with my cell phone to call my dear husband and tell him the happy news.

Too many of my warrior sisters have pulled the dreaded card. To Lynne, Christy, Sue, Patty, Andrea, Ida, Sally and all of the others who continue to fight the fight, I salute you. I also send you my prayers and my love.

The Follow-up Mammogram

By Terry Segal

The fear I try to pant away pierces my heart and jabs at the muscles in my scapula like a bony finger. Someone has crept into this waiting room at Alpharetta Women's Imaging Center and stolen all the air. I breathe like a Georgia bulldog at noon on an August day.

The only man in this BREASTS ONLY ward moves his lips to form the words he silently reads from his novel on the Civil War. We women are at war, too. And it's not so civil. We fight the war against breast cancer and the war within ourselves. We're forced to be both men and women in this world, while we push aside time to play as the children we also are. That makes our breasts tired and they drag on the ground.

The Alpharetta woman with the diamond tennis bracelet sits down too close to me.

Her liposuctioned hips make mine feel chubby against hers. She'd better not suck what little air I have to breathe or I'll smash her like a tennis ball. What magazine article is she reading in *Points North*? "*Forty Uses for Pumpkins.*" I like her now.

That large woman in the cotton candy-colored shirt with the too-tight capris needs to lose weight. She can't be healthy. And why does she perm her hair? She looks like her own grandmother, whom I'm sure I've never met.

Oh—another man. He's here with a woman who states aloud, "I don't want to be here!" As if we do. She holds his arm so tightly he might have to go in with her and have his chest slammed in the glass sliding doors, too.

And that dear woman in the corner seat has had a mastectomy. God bless her.

The technician emerges and taunts me by calling out names that begin with the same letter as mine. People wonder why they hear Cherokee Indian drumming over the cheery 70's "Do the Hustle" music. I don't tell them that it's my heart, running a race with itself. Like feet pounding the pavement. Fear. Fine. Fear. Fine. I lose. I win. I lose. I win.

She called my name.

"Stand up," I tell myself. "Speak, that you are here!"

The command from my brain is received slowly. She walks over to me, and in a voice as sweet as the syrup at IHOP, she says, "Hi. I'm Judy, and I'll be your technician today."

"Hi, Judy. I'll have the Caesar salad."

"Would you like chicken breasts with that?"

"No, thanks. I'll keep my own."

Have they accidentally put me in the morgue? It's freezing in here. Everything is steel and it's darker than my thoughts. Thank goodness Judy uses tooth whiteners. At least I can see her.

Bi-lateral ultrasound first. Okay. Judy just smeared warm apple jelly on both of my breasts. That takes me back to my college years. John used to do that.

Whoa! Are those black areas on the screen considered negative space in your world, Judy? She utters a robotic phrase she's over-rehearsed.

"I'm recording your data and the radiologist will be in to interpret it."

I want to slap her! But just once and not too hard because she did smile at me earlier.

She places two washcloths over me, like doilies on her end tables, and leaves. Just walks out like a lover whom I've disappointed. No drama. No fanfare. Just leaves. I look down to make sure she hasn't tagged my toe.

Nope.

"The drumming can be heard in here, too," I say to myself.

Oh, that's right. It's me.

She came back! Hey, Judy, maybe I'm not so easy to leave.

She tells *me* to go.

Go where? Go to hell?

Go home? Really?

No threatened harpoon service that will suck out the fluid and possibly also my long-term memories? No? Hmmm. Imagine that.

Suddenly, the guilty bastard who stole the oxygen comes back in and fills the room again.

Ahhhhh. Air.

Deep breaths.

Fine breasts.

See you next year.

Coat of Many Colors

By Brooks Dumas

Miss Emmaline climbed out of the church van and kicked past a mongrel dog sniffing trash and debris, searching for his breakfast on the littered sidewalk. He lifted his leg in salute to the trashcan, then shuffled on, while sleepy downtown Main Street in Canton slept off the frenzy of the night before.

It was hot. She tried not to inhale the steamy odors of the street. The heat of the wasteland wrung perspiration from her underarms, leaving dark circles on her dull, green cotton dress. Miss Emmaline looked around the street. *I wouldn't be a bit surprised to see old Satan himself pop his head out of that manhole, lookin' for a sinner like me.*

Out of nowhere a dust devil kicked up and peppered her ankles with sand. She clasped her billowing skirt and took a step. A sheet of newspaper wrapped itself around her calf. Miss Emmaline bent to disentangle herself, but her arms wouldn't extend beyond her generous girth, so she entered the store alternately walking with her right leg and kicking with her left to dislodge the paper.

The bell on the shop door announced her arrival, and Miss Emmaline adjusted her eyes to the interior light. *Every time a bell rings an angel gets its wings.* She took a breath, took a moment to gather her wits about her, and took in her surroundings. There were colors everywhere. She had never seen so many colors. A rack of combs in neon pinks, yellows, and oranges caught her eye. Tubes of makeup, boxes of beauty aides, rainbows of plastic capes, and bonnets were neatly displayed.

"God forgive me," Miss Emmaline said breathlessly to herself, "but this is a most wondrous house of vanity."

The rack of barrettes snagged a memory from her childhood. When she was little, her Daddy had given her a see-through plastic purse with green, red, and blue barrettes. The gift was her reward for shelling a whole bushel of peas all by herself. Daddy had laughed and told her how cute she was, wearing all the barrettes at once.

Oh, how she and her daddy had loved color! Since her daddy went away, she was all alone in this monochrome world, the wife of the Reverend James T. of Birmingham Community Nondenominational Church. Sometimes she saw herself living in a sepia photo, aging, blending further and further into the background, barely visible, just a shadow.

The bangle bracelets on the clerk's arms jingled above the hum of the window unit air-conditioner as she filed away at her long nails. "If I can hep you, honey, you just holler. You lookin' for anything special?"

Miss Emmaline smiled her sweetest preacher's wife smile, but there was something about that gum-chewing, nail-filing, big-haired clerk lady she didn't trust. She usually didn't like flashy women, because mostly they just wanted to steal someone else's husband, and this one was definitely flashy. *Oh yes. I seen your kind in the church congregation.* Miss Emmaline squinted, trying to read the clerk's name badge, but her eyes blurred from the effort. James T. always said calling someone by his given name was important in church. Miss Emmaline reckoned she'd just have to call her "Miss" if she needed her, but disdainfully she thought of her as Miss Jingle Bracelets.

"Where you keep the hair dye?" Miss Emmaline asked, disguising the way she felt with the meek tone of voice she used so often to deceive the church ladies.

The clerk directed her to a long shelf against the left wall. Miss Emmaline walked the aisle, studying the names of the colors of dye: Saucy Beige, Torch, Chocolate Kiss. Woo, she loved them all.

Color had made her feel so special when she was a child, just like Joseph in the Bible must have felt when he first saw his coat of many colors. One time Daddy had come by the house and surprised her and her twin sister Dolly with peacock feathers from Grandma's farm in Ball Ground. Dolly dragged her feathers through the mud and dipped them in ink to try to write with them, but Emmaline had lovingly tied hers together with a sunshine-yellow hair ribbon and stood them in the corner of her room. Emmaline had loved those iridescent blue and green feathers, every single one of them, until Mama made her share them with Dolly. *It didn't matter that Dolly ruined her own feathers. Oh, no. All Dolly had to do was cry to get her way. Everybody always feels sorry for poor, pitiful Dolly. Well, her day's acomin'. She's gonna have to answer to the Lord. Just like the rest of us. Just like I'm gonna have to answer to James T. if I don't get on home.*

Emmaline chose an armful of hair dye boxes. She decided to gather all the colors she liked first, make her choice, then put the unwanted boxes back. She couldn't decide which one to keep. She wanted all of them. God forgive her, she needed all of them. She needed some color in her life again.

Clasping her purse and her hair dye boxes to her bosoms, Miss Emmaline started toward the counter. The clerk looked up from her nail filing and said, "Well, honey, I was worried about you standin' back there all this time, but it looks like you found some purty colors." She gestured to the shelves with her silvery nail file. "There's somethin' to please everbody on them shelves, to my way of thinkin'."

Miss Emmaline didn't quite know what to say to the saucy Miss Jingle Bracelets, so she slipped into her meekest voice. "I just couldn't decide. On a color, you know."

The clerk lady hurried from behind the counter and took Miss Emmaline by the elbow, directing her back toward the hair dye aisle. "Looka here, honey. I told ya I'd hep ya. That's what I'm here for. Color choosin' is my specialty. This here's called Ruby," she said as she plumped her own shoulder length tresses. *Jingle, Jingle, Jingle.* "It says on the box it's a red-violet. I just love it. Don't you? Until I get tired of it. Then I'll choose another color if I take a notion to. You know what I mean? Now what color did you have in mind, honey? Blond? Red?"

Miss Emmaline didn't have any color in mind. She had chosen each color because of the tempting name on the box. Whatever color she ended up with would suit her fine, as long as it was shiny, instead of dull mousy brown, but she didn't want to admit that to this woman. "I don't know. I...somethin' not too noticeable. My husband says he likes my hair just the way it is."

"Oh, honey, that's what they all say. Once they got you. My man wanted to keep me locked up in the kitchen cookin' or in the bedroom makin' babies. I told him, 'huh, uh. I'm not your mama. I'm your little sweet potato.' I aint givin' him no excuse for sleepin' around. You hear me? I make sure I'm all the woman he needs. If he wants a blonde, I can be a blonde. If he wants a redhead, I can be a redhead."

Miss Emmaline never thought of it that way, but it made sense to her.

"Now let's see about you. Let's start you out with somethin' close to your hair color? Somethin' in ash brown might be just the thang. Here's one. It's called "Pretty Beaver." If this don't make your husband worship you like a goddess, my name's not Jeri Sue."

A bubble of defiance welled up in Emmaline's chest. *Well, Miss Jeri Sue Jingle Bracelets, I want them all, and I shall have them all, too, Missy.* She pretended to study the boxes in her arms, and said mildly, "I think I want to take all these and decide onct I get home. If I keep my receipt, I can bring back the ones I don't want. Cain't I?"

She spilled her boxes of hair dye onto the counter and began to rifle in her purse for the envelope containing the choir-robe money collected during last night's choir practice. The clerk's words were ringing like warning bells in her head. *Makin' babies and girlfriends and the name of that hair-dye color.* She just wouldn't think about that now. James T. always said thinking would get her in trouble one day. Besides, she was tired of caring what other people thought.

"If I's ta pay ya everything I owe ya, all at onct, how much would that be?" She paid for the purchase and tuned out the clerk who was busy jingling, talking, making change, and putting all the boxes in a paper sack.

This life I'm living sure ain't what I deserve. Miss Emmaline got angry just thinking about her sacrifices. *Does the congregation ever pay me for my service to them? No, they do not. Do they even appreciate me? No, m'am, they do not. Just smilin' and keepin' my mouth shut when I want to scream at them and pull out their hair is worth something...is worth a lot. Besides, I deserve to be beautiful. It must say somewhere in the Bible, "Thou must beautify thyself unto the Lord." If it doesn't say those exact words, there has to be a passage to that effect somewhere in the Holy Book. James T. is always able to find passages to justify his sins, even though he reminds me daily that I need to repent for mine. Well, I choose to take my chances with sin. It isn't the first time, and it probably won't be the last. I reckon I can always color my hair and repent later. That's like everybody else in the congregation. They act the fool all week long and beg God and James T. for forgiveness on the Sabbath, like nothin' ever happened. Yes, ma'am, a new hair color is exactly what I need.*

"Anything else for you today, honey?" The clerk eyed her curiously. Her usual customers were bright birds of a feather, ready to preen, paint, and color their plumage. This poor little sparrow would never survive the streets. Too dull.

"No thank you. You was a big help." Emmaline shouldered her purse strap, hefted the paper bag in her arms, and left the store. Now that the deed was done, her stomach felt a little jumpy. She had spent most of the choir money, but those old fools would never miss it. If they did, she'd tell them she didn't know where the money went. No one questioned the preacher's wife. Did they? She could just replace the money from the collection plate before James T. had a chance to count it. That always worked before. *Praise the Lord.*

All the way back to Birmingham Community, Miss Emmaline grumbled out loud. "If I had somewhere to go, I'd for sure just keep on driving, right past that church, and on down the road." She looked at the boxes of dye in the sack beside her. "I'd change my hair color every week. Miss Jingle Bracelets wouldn't have nothin' on me."

The only time she ever really felt alive was when she and James T. "changed churches." Miss Emmaline would never tell him how exciting their middle of the night flights were. Out the back door they would go with only the clothes on their backs, leaving behind all the hypocrites and self-righteous old biddies that really ran the church. They would load themselves into the new Cadillac the church had given them and drive noiselessly out of town. She thought James T. secretly liked the thrill of the run, too. Even though he pretended to scowl angrily, leaving had always been a chance for him to start over, to flee some clinging woman who had worked her wiles on him or some irate husband who blamed him for the sins of the wife.

The van rumbled along between the ruts of the dirt driveway. She parked behind the white clapboard church, the church James T. had felt called to move to four years ago after their last church burned. *What a glorious night that was! All the church goers cryin' and wailin' like the Lord took His valuable time to reign down fire and brimstone on their heads. Fools! I doubt the Lord really cared enough to burn down their dusty old church anyhow. I expect the Lord, like me, secretly enjoyed the bright yellows, reds, and oranges of them pretty flames shootin' toward heaven like some glorious sacrificial pyre. Hallelujah.*

The parsonage was silent when Miss Emmaline went inside. In the adjoining bedroom, James T. snored softly, sleeping off his lunch. His diamond cross-shaped pinky ring rested on the night table beside him. She nudged it with her index finger as she walked by.

Miss Emmaline quietly closed the bathroom door and switched on the light. Her pale skin looked green and her hair was as dull as a matted dog's coat under the glare of the bathroom's fluorescent. How had she lost her color? James T. said color was the work of the devil. "Mark my words," James T. had said, "people who wear all them colors is just looking for attention, and that," he punctuated his pronouncement as only James T. could do, "is the sin of vanity."

Emmaline hid the boxes of hair dye in the storage closet behind the extra rolls of toilet tissue. Later, she'd dig out the boxes, and choose a hair color when he was out ministering to his flock. She turned off the light and quietly tiptoed into the bedroom to stash her other package in the back of the bedroom closet. Inside were two identical pale blue dresses with tiny blue flowers and tiny white lace collars, one for her, one for her twin sister Dolly. When James T. got up from his nap, she was on the back porch drinking a cool glass of iced tea.

*   *   *   *

Sister Dolly sat on the front row of the church beside Miss Emmaline. Both sisters had on white gloves and straw hats. Their "Sunday-Go-To-Meetin" outfits this Sunday were their new blue dresses Miss Emmaline had gotten from the Sears store at North Point Mall in Alpharetta. Emmaline's head was down, seemingly in prayer, but she was really staring at her puffy ankles crossed in front of her. Every Sunday her body was there on that hard pew, but her mind was wishing she was somewhere else.

"He that liveth in pleasure is dead while he yet liveth." James T.'s words burned through the fog of her wandering mind. *You always seem to know what I'm up to, James T.* Emmaline watched him fidget with his cross-shaped pinky ring. *You choose just the right Bible verse to shame me, don't you? Sometimes I swear I don't know where God's words end and yours begin.*

"Are you ready to trust the King of Kings, the Lord of Lords?"

Trust? She looked up at the choir sweltering in their heavy, faded robes. A few choir members tried to calm restless babies. Others sat stoically in the heat, waiting for the next hymn. They would have been cooler in their new summer robes, if they hadn't trusted Miss Emmaline with their money.

How many of these women have you trusted with your special blessing, James T? She glanced at Sister Dolly sitting beside her. *Even you, my very own twin sister, couldn't resist his divine power. Seems like you always want everything, and seems like you always get it. You got every penny of Aunt Liffey's worldly goods. What makes everyone want to look after you? What about me once in a while?*

Anger had burned through her when she first found out about the Aunt Liffey's inheritance, but, like a good daughter of God, she had given up her anger to prayer. She had prayed all night to be granted understanding and to learn forgiveness. At first light an answer to her prayers had come to her. An epiphany. *God helps those who help themselves.*

The fans droned on overhead, stirring the hot air in the church. In spite of the stream of sweat that trickled down her back, Miss Emmaline smiled. She knew if she were bound for Hell, she'd love the fire and hate the heat. She straightened her skirt and pulled at her slip, which was stuck to her legs. Sister Dolly fanned herself with the paper fan advertising Alpharetta Peaceful Rest Funeral Home, and James T. preached on.

"The word of God says in the last days you will be called before the judges." James T. seemed to point directly at Miss Emmaline and Sister Dolly. "Say 'amen' if you know the power of the Lord, and give the Lord a clap offering."

The sisters and brothers amened and clapped their hands. Filled with the frenzy of James T.'s words, they all stood up swaying and waving their arms to the music of the choir, which, as if by some silent cue, had begun to sing.

"Brother and Sisters, I know you been troubled."

"Amen," the choir sang.

"Amen," Miss Emmaline said under her breath.

James T. stepped down into the aisle, and the music stopped. The churchgoers stood still, hungering for his next words.

"I'm healed by the power of God, and the devil don't like that," his words boomed into the rafters of the church. "He can heal you too. Shake my hand if the Lord healed you, brothers and sisters."

He made his way down the aisle, shaking hands, his cross-shaped pinky ring twinkling on his finger. Behind him Brother Alvin and Brother Rayford passed the collection plate amongst the good people of Birmingham Community Church.

Like the handmaiden of the Lord, Miss Emmaline had slipped down the side aisle to do her duty. She stood at the back of the church under the heavy wooden cross suspended from the balcony. Every Sunday she locked the collection money in the church office during the final prayer and waited for James T. at the church door to shake hands with the congregation. Every Sunday she smiled meekly, like a cardboard cutout of a preacher's wife, and listened to the parishioners praise James T.'s words of salvation as they filed out of church. Every Sunday she prayed that the words of The Good Book would give her patience for one more Sunday. *Wait on the Lord and keep His way and you will inherit the land.*

*   *   *   *

It was misting rain. The graveside rites were said. The funeral was over. James T. thought about his poor Miss Emmaline lying in the coldness of the earth's embrace, burned beyond recognition. His congregation surrounded him, like sheep around their shepherd, offering the comfort of their nearness.

Lord, how could you take Miss Emmaline in the church fire? James T. shook his head in puzzlement. *Two of my churches burned to the ground. Hmm, hmm, hmm.* There were so many unanswered questions. He knew Miss Emmaline had met her sister at the church two nights ago to say goodbye. He knew there was a fire. Miss Emmaline could have gotten out this time, too, if only that heavy wooden cross hadn't broken loose and fallen from the balcony, striking her in the head. *She just lay there, poor soul, 'til fire and smoke consumed her.* Beyond that, he didn't know anything else. He sought comfort in the words of the Bible. *The Lord giveth, and the Lord taketh away.* James T. wiped his eyes with his starched white handkerchief. Unconsciously, he massaged his little finger searching for the comfort of the warm gold of his pinky ring. He was all alone without his partner in life, Miss Emmaline. He had tried to reach Sister Dolly to tell her that her sister was dead. Perhaps they could have comforted each other, but it was too late. Sister Dolly was on a bus somewhere, headed to her aunt's house in Arizona. He would write to tell her the sad news about Emmaline's death as soon as God gave him the right words to say.

*   *   *   *

The darkness of the late-night Greyhound surrounded her. In her sweet blue dress she looked just like her sister had the last time she saw her, standing under the wooden cross in the back of the church. Leaving her sister made her feel a little sad, but they would see each other again one day, in God's good time. Anyhow, she'd think about her sister in the morning. Right now she breathed a deep sigh, glad to be finally on her way. Thank heaven for Aunt Liffey's house in Arizona, her very own inherited spot of Paradise. *The Lord works in mysterious ways, His wonders to perform.*

She had collected enough money in her pocketbook to buy a bus ticket. She could sing a chorus of praises to the Lord for that too. In Arizona, the lawyer was holding Aunt Lif's money for her. She could be independent at last.

She fingered the cross shape of the ring on the chain around her neck, the ring James T. had given her. Well, he hadn't actually given it to her, but he would want her to have it. From time to time she glanced at her reflection in the bus window. Her shiny brown hair seemed to frame her face with an almost holy aura. She thought she looked like one of those saints in the pictures that decorated the church hall. The rhythm of the bus lulled her to sleep, and she dreamed she was an angel winging her way to heaven through the fiery colors of the sunset. *Amen.*

Learning to Live Together

By Carolyn Robbins

"Jared, where is my pink curler bag?" snapped his sweet wife of two weeks.

Jared stared at the bathroom door in shock. "Uh, I think you might've told me to throw it out?"

"No, I said, *not* to throw it out."

"Oh."

"'Oh!' Is that all you can say? Right now, I want you to retrieve that bag or at least its contents."

"Honey, it looked so worn out."

"That's because I use it. Where is it?"

"Gone."

"Gone!" He heard her draw in a deep breath, causing him to take an involuntary step backward into the dresser. The lamp swayed erratically and he grabbed it moments before it would have crashed to the floor.

Her measured words floated back. "Then you'll have to go to the store."

"I can't go to the store now. The Falcons' game starts in fifteen minutes and?"

"You threw out my bag and now you have to replace them."

"Them? What them?"

"You idiot! That bag held my tampons. I can't go anywhere now."

"Don't you have spares in your purse?"

"Had is the operative word. I used them all. I thought I had a whole box in my curler bag."

Jared glanced at the clock; he had only thirteen minutes until the kick-off. "But, but, I can't go buy tampons."

An icy pause permeated the air between them. "Why in the world not?"

"The Falcons are the play-offs for the first time in ten years, and I, I don't want to be seen with tampons," he blurted.

"It's the eighties not the fifties. You're a liberated man. You can do this."

"But, the game."

"The store is at the corner of Roswell and Abernathy. You'll be back in time if you go now."

Jared entered Kroger in less than five minutes, and headed for the beer section. He needed more than the two cans he had in his refrigerator. Besides, if he had more than one item in his cart, the damn tampons wouldn't stand out. Right? Well, maybe.

He placed two six-packs in the bottom and wheeled past the chips. On impulse he grabbed two bags of pretzels, and practically ran to the toilet paper aisle. His plan of cruising through, casually grabbing a box, and walking nonchalantly to the register crashed and burned. There were no Tampax boxes in sight.

"Where the hell do they keep these things?" he muttered under his breath. He went up one aisle after another. At one point he considered asking a gray-haired employee whose nametag read Max. But Max was talking to some woman with three little kids. Then, at last, he found them sitting next to the shampoo. He slid the damn box under the pretzels and proceeded to the checkout line.

He checked his watch. The game was starting in four minutes. He loaded all his items on the conveyer belt and complimented himself on picking the fastest checker in the store. With all his cash in his hand, he waited to pay. Even though he had casually arranged the Tampax box between the two bags of pretzels, it became the lone item on the belt when the cashier picked up both bags and rang them up together. Then she picked up the box and turned it over and over, looking for the price.

Great, he thought, let's hold it up for everyone to see what I'm buying.

Moving a wad of gum into her cheek, she asked, "Do you remember the price?"

Jared stammered, "Uh, no."

She grabbed the intercom, it cracked and whined with age. She yelled, "Max, I need a price on Tampax."

Jared flushed and looked at the woman behind him, he mumbled, "Sorry."

He watched the line of impatient shopper grow to five more baskets. The checker quickly bagged all his groceries, oblivious of his discomfort. Finished, she grabbed the microphone again. It immediately started howling. She tapped it once, and it spit out a softer static hiss. She said, "Max, do you have that Tampax price yet?"

"I'm getting it. It takes a while to get to the other side."

She frowned. "Why does he have to go across the store?"

The response resounded for everyone to hear. "What kind have you got? American or that foreign stuff?"

"What are you talking about?"

"There's a lot of 'em. Do you want room temperature or from the cooler. I prefer them cool so they don't foam over the side."

"What?"

"Well, is it Michelob or Corona, or??"

Everyone in the line burst into laughter. The cashier shouted back. "You deaf old coot, not six-packs, Tampax."

I Learned Two Deaths Today

By Marre Dangar Stevens

I learned two deaths today.

One full of age and honor.

One young and empty with self-defeat.

After a hundred years,

Granny gently went to sleep,

Having done something useful

For someone else

Every day of her life.

After thirty years,

Sharon stacked her makeup and clothing bills

With a note: "I can never be free of all these debts."

With one shot,

She was.

Literary Lines

By Jordan Segal

I'm sitting in my room
With paper by my side
The rubric lists requirements
For thoughts I feel inside.

I'm supposed to write a poem
With twenty lines or more
It needs alliteration,
Rhyme and metaphor.

It's now 3 a.m.
The day before it's due
My teacher's gonna kill me
I must add a rhyme or two.

Alliteration next
I neither knew nor know
What's that I hear? My chime goes off
And now it's time to go.

One more thing that's on my list
Before I leave for school
A metaphor is all I need
But wait, what is that rule?

Metaphors are hard to find
I'm crazy in the head
I think I would be better off
With simile instead.

At Roswell High, it's gonna be
A kick-butt, awesome day
Because this poem's like gold to me
I'd better get an A!

The Choice

By Michael Buchanan

Each spring, my high school trigonometry classes build and launch bottle-rockets and we read the book *October Sky*. When we first started reading the biography, I borrowed the media center's digital camera because I thought no one would believe that a math class was reading a book. I needed evidence. Unfortunately, by the time I made it back to the library, it was closed. So, I trekked back to my portable classroom, thinking of what to do with the expensive item. Taking it home with me was certainly not an option; I didn't want to be responsible. In my trailer was, I thought, a secure room between the two adjoining classrooms, so I put the camera in there and locked the door.

Returning the next day, I was disgusted to discover the doorframe broken and the camera missing. It was very difficult to tell the librarians that I had lost their $800 camera. After that conversation, I figured I would be lucky if I could borrow a pencil. Also gone were the pictures of the class but those at least could be re-created. Nothing of my own was stolen even though I did have a nice radio and CDs in there. After the initial shock and the realization that there wasn't much I could do, life went on but with a slightly more cynical twist. Even still, I tried to read the faces of all the students I came in contact with to see if they ratted themselves out but no face held indisputable evidence.

Later that year, mostly due to the peak time of the cyclical sunspot activity, I took my telescope to school. Using a solar filter, we tracked sunspots for several days. My students thought this was interesting, and it allowed me to bring life to more applications of the math I teach. Since the trailers were to be used minimally that summer, I left the telescope in the closet at school. An old cumbersome relic, it still worked well but did not give the slightest appearance of value. Its box was water-stained and faded while the cushions inside were so dry that a gentle touch caused disintegration.

Upon arriving back for pre-planning of the following year, I was greeted with a crumpled and damaged telescope box. My heart sank and my blood pressure doubled when I pulled back the cardboard flaps to discover my telescope missing. The one that, twenty-five years earlier, I had scrimped and saved what I could of my teacher's salary to buy. And now, it was gone. At that moment, my heart felt as empty and as tattered as the box. Later, students of mine from the previous year stopped by to say hello and I told them my story. They offered compassion and a promise to spread the word of my situation. I told the school administrators and resource officer, but there was nothing they could do because the item was personal. As the week moved along, I couldn't shake a distrustful attitude. Finally, I resigned myself to accept one more disheartening event and to discover other ways of bringing the wonders of the heavens to my classroom.

When the first week of school started, the previous disappointments lingered but bright new faces deserved my attention and concerns. The second day of the year started no different from many others. The routine was a cup of coffee, a granola bar, and a walk through the connecting portion of the trailer to visit my friend next door. In this small room sat the telescope box, broken and exhausted. This time, however, I noticed a small envelope carefully taped to the top flap of the five-foot-long container. Disjointed, different colored sentences were written upon it. The first one I read was scrawled across the top in purple pencil. It stated simply in block letters, "FIX IT UP WITH THIS $". Along the bottom were words that, despite the poor handwriting, revealed a conscience reaching out. "eVeRY ONe makes a Choice iN life, a CHANGE in life style" was there to help me understand what I was about to find. In the envelope was $50 in wrinkled fives and tens. As I pulled back the top of the box, somehow I knew what I would see. And it was *there*. My telescope was back. Scratched up a little and probably needing minor repair, but it was back. Considerate, careful hands had attempted to put all the pieces where they thought each item belonged. And it had happened under the cover of darkness. Someone had broken into my trailer to bring something back that meant so much to me. Rushing down the hall, I couldn't wait to tell our school officer about this discovery. In looking at the envelope, we both wondered at the significance of a hand-drawn arrow, two eyes and the words "sony back." Suddenly, it dawned on me what they meant. Interrupting a class, I sprinted into the room where the telescope lay and placed the envelope back in its original position. I followed the arrow and looked to where it directed me. In silent testimony for the heart of the accused and resting on a stack of papers, sat the digital camera and its charger.

I never found out who stole, and returned, the camera and my telescope. And, I never asked. I didn't need to. Tucked in the corner of the envelope was one word; "sorry." A heart redeemed gives each of us hope.

Chinese Zodiac

By John Sheffield

From kindergarten through fourth grade, my best friend was Wanda Chang. When her family moved from Roswell to Seattle, I moped around the house for weeks. But Wanda left me with something wonderful. For her seventh birthday, in April 1985, she invited me to celebrate with her family at a Chinese restaurant. To my young eyes, it was a palace with its ornate lanterns and colorful paintings. To crown it all, in front of me at the table, a place mat showed strange pictures of animals.

"What's this?" I asked.

"Our Chinese twelve-year zodiac, Naomi," Mr. Chang replied. "It tells your fortune. See how under each picture there are dates and a description of your personality and attributes."

"When were you born?" Wanda's mother asked.

"February seventh, 1978," I replied.

"My goodness, I think you were born on the Chinese New Year's Day," Wanda's father exclaimed. "I remember, because Wanda was also born in seventy-eight. To be safe, I'll check the date with Mrs. Liu, the owner. It's tricky, our new year's date depends on the phase of the moon. If I'm right, you were born on the first day of the Year of the Horse. If the year started later in 1978, you would be a snake."

"I'd prefer to be a horse," I exclaimed.

"I hope you are," said Wanda. "I'm a horse."

When Mr. Chang returned, he said, "Mrs. Liu says it was February seventh. That's very auspicious."

Back then, I didn't know what auspicious meant, but it sounded grand. "My dad says I was the first baby born at the hospital that day," I said. "He had to rush Mom and me in all of a sudden."

"Even more auspicious," said Mr. Chang. "We must have a toast." We all raised our glasses to celebrate me and Wanda being horses.

As we left, I folded the paper place mat and hid it under my tee-shirt.

When I got home, I told my mom and dad about being born in the Year of the Horse, and they thought it was funny. Because New Year's Day moved around, I didn't mention that my birthday was the actual day. I was very careful who I made friends with, because we horses are friendly mainly to tigers and dogs, but never to rats. It wasn't easy, because the nearest Years of the Tiger were 1974 and 1986, and for dogs they were 1970 and 1982. The Zodiac didn't say anything about horses having relationships with snakes, 1977, or sheep, 1979, so I guessed they were okay.

My dad framed the place mat and it hung above the small desk in my bedroom. For my next birthday, my mom gave me a book about the Chinese Zodiac. I consulted it regularly when I needed to make decisions. I was certain of one thing, horses were wonderful, and I pestered my parents about learning to ride. In 1980, they gave in. To be honest, I wasn't very good and fell off a lot, but I knew it was the right thing for me.

My younger brother was born in April 1984—the Year of the Rat. At first I liked him, but my parents spoiled him and as he grew older we didn't get on, proving the Chinese were right. I stayed away from him, and when my arm healed from my latest fall, I spent more time riding. That was until the next time I fell off and got a concussion. Then my parents decided I should give up riding for a bit, but I still went to the stables to talk to the horses.

My secret and I got along fine until college, where I met a graduate student named George and fell in love immediately. Unfortunately, he was born in 1972, the Year of the Rat. We got on wonderfully well. But, in my heart, I knew it could never be, and I broke up with him. I was heartbroken and began to lose faith in the system. Then I met Henry, another graduate student, who was born at the end of 1971, the Year of the Pig. I knew he wasn't a tiger or a dog, but at least he wasn't a rat. Pigs and horses live together on farms and I was sure they got on well. When Henry proposed, I accepted. We set the wedding for February seventh, my birthday.

Unlike most brides, I wasn't late getting to the church, and my dad and I had to wait outside for a few minutes until the guests was settled.

"Isn't it great, my getting married on my birthday, Dad?"

"Sure thing, honey, though I guess, strictly, it isn't your actual birthday," Dad replied.

A cold shiver went down my back. "What do you mean?"

"Well, I've told you how I had to rush your mother to the hospital and we only just made it in time. I helped deliver you in the car just after we arrived outside the emergency room."

"Yes, I know. But what?—"

"I'm sure I told you that it took quite a long time to get someone to register your birth, and by then it was the seventh. You're mother and I decided not to make a big deal out of it. They'd already—"

Before Dad could finish, an usher came out and told us we needed to go right in.

As we walked up the aisle, I asked, "So when was I born?"

"Just before midnight on the sixth," he replied. "Are you okay, honey?" he added, sensing me slipping from his arm.

"This is terrible," I said. "I'm a snake, and Henry's a pig. This will never work."

"What are you talking about?" said my father as he let go of my arm and turned to face me.

"The Zodiac, of course, Dad," I shouted, as I tore past the flower girl who was daintily dropping rose petals in the aisle.

"Henry, I'm sorry. This won't work." I turned to the wedding guests. "I've got to call this off. I'm not a horse, I'm a snake and Henry's a pig. It's a disaster."

Henry stuttered, "Wha...wha...what are—?"

I put my hand to Henry's face before he could continue. "I'm sorry. It was not meant to be."

As I walked back down the aisle, I could see by the shocked look on all their faces that the guests knew exactly what I was talking about.

Obrero

By Paul A. Bussard

Me llamo Eugenio, but most gringos can't say my name right. I can't criticize them. I can't say my own name right in English. Señora Bassett, the lady who teaches English at the library, told me to say "Cheen," or something like that. She wrote it down for me: G-e-n-e. In Spanish, that would be "Henny." I'll never understand English. No wonder Señora Bassett prays before class.

No importa. I don't need a name anyway or even a face—just a strong back. *Yo soy obrero.* I work when I am chosen. I wait when I am not.

Tengo miedo. Truth is, I been scared ever since I left Mexico—scared coming into the U.S., scared I wouldn't find work, then scared when I did. I got in a truck with a total stranger, had no idea where he was taking me, what he wanted me to do, how much he would pay me, or even *if* he would pay me.

No todos son buenos. Ten men went out on a job last week. They came home late, and I knew something was wrong. The men were silent and everyone was looking at Alejandro. As soon as he got out of the van, he started throwing rocks at the back of the gas station where they'd been picked up. He threw them as fast as he could gather them. When there were no more rocks, he threw handfuls of dirt. I heard *mierda* and *hijo de puta* and a few other words. Carlos went to get him, but he knew not to touch Alejandro—just talked to him quietly and waited. Alejandro was worn out—all of the men were—and they went as a group into the pool hall. I followed.

It seems the job took longer than expected, or maybe it was planned that way all along. Whatever. The *jefe* paid nine of them, but ran out of money before paying Alejandro. *El pinche ratero* just shrugged his shoulders and told the other nine to share. Some will, some won't. Not all are *compañeros.* A hundred dollars is a lot of money to us—even divided nine ways—and if Alejandro takes their money, he will be obligated to the others. This is bad. Now Alejandro will go back home and work for the *droguistas.*

Today was a good day for me. Carlos and I worked for a man—*un viejo*—too old to climb a ladder. We brought down boxes from his attic. It was hot work, but he let us rest a lot. He talked to us in broken Spanish and was interested in our troubles—the difficulties in crossing the border, problems with *la policía*, families and conditions in Mexico. It was nice to be treated as a person. *Algunos son simpáticos.*

I miss my family and my home. I will go back soon. I could stay, become an *americano,* and bring my family here, but it would take a long time and *mi abuela* is too old to start over in such a different world. Mexico is our home.

After I return to *la madre patria,* I will start all over again—sneak across the border, hide from the INS, and work my way back here or some other place where I can earn money to send to my family. What else can I do? *Yo soy obrero.*

Song of the Mockingbird

By Kathleen Craft Boehmig

My new bed of flowers glimmered, thirstily drinking in the water from my garden hose. The petunias and blue salvia provided a pleasing contrast to the pastels of tea roses and hydrangeas. Pleased with my efforts, I faced the setting sun that tinted the summer sky a lemon-yellow beyond the giant southern pines and dogwoods in our front yard.

Songbirds called to each other as I watered the garden. It was the time of day for settling-in with mates in a soft, cozy nest for the night; for snuggling down to protect eggs and fuzzy hatchlings.

I smiled, watching two mockingbirds heading for their nest in the tree-tops...but they sounded raucous. To my horror, I saw that a crow had discovered their nest. The parents defended it aggressively, screaming and pecking. Feathers flew. I dropped my garden hose and jumped up and down, yelling and waving my arms; but it was no use. With the distraught mockingbirds in frantic pursuit, their baby's legs dangling from his beak, the predator carried off the hapless little creature.

My shoulders drooped as I picked up the still spewing hose. The parents were already guarding the nest again, and suddenly there was more commotion. The crow was back. And in spite of the birds' hectic frenzy and my own efforts, the invader snatched another baby mockingbird from its nest.

It's hopeless, I thought. All the babies are doomed. Who was I to think I could—or should—intervene? Wasn't this all part of nature's brutal, glorious, gory way? Well, I decided, not if I could help it. Not in my front yard.

It was the timeless struggle of the ages: man trying to control his environment. We have such a short time here on earth, and we forget that we are stewards, not owners, of the land we inhabit. We want to leave a lasting legacy, to say: "I was here. Look what I accomplished." The crux of all our efforts, if possible, would be to thwart death—the ultimate thing we can't do.

I kept watch while I continued watering the garden. And here came the crow again. The mockingbird parents launched into their defense mode, and this time I had another trick up my sleeve. I turned the water on its most powerful jet and aimed it into the tree between the marauding crow and the nest, then twirled the hose so it looked like a spiraling geyser.

The crow hovered in midair, then retreated. But for how long, I wondered? I couldn't stand out here all night screaming, dancing around and twirling the hose over my head. But I couldn't rest indoors, knowing that those baby birds were in danger. So I remained at my post for another half-hour as the twilight deepened.

The crow returned twice more. Each time the attacker approached, the mockingbird parents and I would defend the nest. The crow finally flew off down the street and through the woods. The mockingbirds were silent, probably cuddling their remaining babies.

As I cleaned up, I reflected on the experience. I knew every helpless creature couldn't be saved. And they were just wild birds…birds that only exist for a few years; creatures that do nothing but flit about eating, raising baby birds and singing.

Tears stung my eyes. Their singing, for me, is the chief charm of all our songbirds. In spite of their territorial struggles, the main thrust of their presence in my harried life is their addition of song and beauty. Whenever I heard birdsong, I felt blessed. And the least I could do was to defend them when presented with the opportunity. Even though we couldn't outsmart death or nature, I mused, we could win some little battles.

So, I asked myself, where should we draw the deus-ex-machina line? Was my participation just an egotistic attempt to exert control over my environment? Was God laughing at me in my pitiful dancing outrage? I didn't think so. It had to do with that stewardship which He assigned us.

And, I wondered, when my stewardship is over, what then, when I'm gone? Will a shadow in my shape dance in the golden sunset light, twirling spirals of shadow-spray into the dusk? Will birds trill notes that sound like "Kathleen"? Will a sound like my voice whisper stories of winged flight in children's dreams? And will my native Georgia clay bear the starry hearts of flowers I planted for generations to come? In the words of Whitman, "The powerful play goes on, and you may contribute a verse." What will my verse be?

About ten days later, I was walking down my driveway admiring the garden in the morning light when I heard a plaintive cry. A fledgling mockingbird was perched on top of our mailbox.

I stood quietly as he looked me up and down. Still regarding me, the young bird threw his head back and warbled twice: two avian syllables. He then flew to his parent and gave me no further notice.

But I whistled as I walked back to the house. The fledgling had sung my verse from the powerful play: my legacy lies in the song of the mockingbird.

A Good Idea—But Whose?

By Cecilia Branhut

"How much longer are you going to live in an apartment? You do realize you're throwing good money after bad. Maybe you're not interested in a tax break…"

I'd been hearing this from knowing friends for too long, but I didn't pay serious attention. Suddenly, however, another voice was taking over. To this day I can't explain who—or even what—it was, but I was led, as if on a leash, to call the only realtor I knew.

"Sean, let's look at condos."

Sean has the gift of calm and acceptance. He showed no surprise, just went about the business of putting together a few possibilities, and off we went one Saturday. I lived in Dunwoody, worked in Alpharetta, so we headed north on Georgia 400. We must have looked at four or five places that first day, with one or two vaguely appealing to me.

Sean took me to lunch. "OK, now you've seen some of what's out there. Do you have a better picture of what you have in mind?" he asked in his light Irish brogue.

I peered at him through my mental fog. "Are you kidding!" I said. "I have nothing in mind, but I sense I'll know what I like when I see it." I'm not sure Sean believed me, or even if I believed myself.

But, miraculously it happened, in Alpharetta, the very next weekend. There wasn't a strong Aha!, because the seller's daughter and family had trashed the place, but once again that "something else" took over, tightened the leash, and said through my voice, "I think this is it."

"It" was an end unit (no one above, no one below, only someone behind a firewall to one side) in an older condominium complex whose buildings were nestled among trees and bushes, even though, in that frigid winter, the true lushness was yet to be revealed.

Then began the business process, again through which I sailed in a daze. I'd never bought a home by myself, so I depended totally on Sean's knowledge and contacts. Now I'm a real pro and would never do that again, but hindsight enjoys 20-20 vision.

At Sean's recommendation—and I still love him in spite of everything, having maturely realized he's a businessman and not the Red Cross—I used his mortgage broker, who arrived at the closing with an interest rate higher than the one we'd agreed upon (he knew a dope when he saw one).

"Why is that?" I asked. As I recall, his reply was fuzzy, while Sean, who was there for moral support (whose?), and the attorney remained silent.

My same trusty realtor acquaintance (by this time I'd temporarily demoted Sean from friend) then steered me to a carpet company from hell. They, too, knew a dope when they saw one.

And so it went, through my own selection of a moving company—pretty good, except for the owner's defensiveness and impatience with me—and Lowe's (yes, I'll name them) who replaced, to my satisfaction, two abused, broken appliances and one toilet (how do you manage to break an entire toilet?!).

Was it all worth the upheaval, the anxiety, and the odd sensation of being outside myself looking in? My contentment with my new home in Alpharetta is secure in spite of the clogging rush-hour traffic and the murderous felling of trees to make way for more restaurants, more stores, more offices, and more homes to house more residents.

However, the developers of my twenty-year-old condominium community must have been tree-huggers like me, or at least not wanton decimators of plant- and tree-life. When spring arrives each year, holly, silverberry, Russian olive, evergreen, and magnolia are joined by the competing leaves of oak, sycamore, and so much more. And we're close to charming Downtown Alpharetta, where any new building must conform to the city's historic ambience.

We are also not far from the Alpharetta Senior Center, a delicious oasis for people of a certain age. Fine tennis courts beckon us to play three mornings a week throughout the year, and our enthusiastic, diverse group competes happily, even with Cruella de Ville whom we silently tolerate.

This all begs the question, Why did I spend fifteen years renting an apartment, giving no thought to being a homeowner, paying too much income tax…? Oh, give it a rest!

The Recital

By Terry Segal

What are you looking at?
I want to scream.
You have nothing better to do than show up at
North Atlanta Talent Education for a violin recital?
I scan the eager faces in rows of chairs,
Evenly spaced like seeds on a strawberry.

Okay.
Deep breaths.
Should I tune my gastric juices to A,
Since everyone will hear them over the music?
My knees clang together
Providing a lovely rhythmic accompaniment.
Breathe.

Wait.
I'm inhaling too much and too often.
I'm dizzy.
What if I pass out?
Relax.

Oh my gosh!
I've gone deaf.
I can't hear a thing.
Maybe if I swallow…
I can't swallow!
The fluid is collecting in my mouth
And my tongue won't push it down my throat.
What if I drool during the performance?

Bigger problems present themselves.
My hands are on fire.
No, wait—they're freezing.
They're crystallized popsicles stuck to a napkin.

I can't free them.
Now they're melting ice cubes
That drip in the heat of the day.

Okay.
Take it easy.
Breathe.
No! Not the breathing thing again.
And don't even think about swallowing.

My eyelid is stuck.
I'm not blinking enough.
My aqueous humor has dried up.
I'm all right.
The teacher said,
"Recitals are just about playing music."
Liar!

There's the cue to begin.
There's the first note.
Okay.
Okay.
Who's responsible for the incessant banging
That echoes through the hall?
Oh,
It's my heart threatening to beat its way out of my chest.

Hey…
The music sounds pretty wonderful.
See?
This isn't so bad.

I'm just glad that it's my child, not me, performing today.

Pick a Flick

By Bobbi Kornblit

I promised myself I wouldn't stop at the Krispy Kreme, even if the neon "hot light" blazed in the front window. Fresh warm donuts weren't what I needed; they'd fill out my thighs but not the hole I felt deep inside me.

My eyes focused straight ahead on Atlanta Street until I finally turned onto the quiet lane in Roswell where my sister and brother-in-law lived. Along the front path, a row of hostas drooped in the summer heat. Sheltered from the rays, I stood on the covered porch and knocked on the front door. I tried the knob and the door opened.

"Anybody home?" I called out, relishing the cool air in the entry hall.

"I'll be ready in a few minutes. What time does the movie start?" Mia shouted from the upstairs bedroom.

"Depends on what we're going to see." I shuffled through the clutter on the coffee table to find a spot to put my purse.

Gerald slid open the pocket doors from his study. "Hi, Rochelle, I didn't know you were here already. What are you up for seeing tonight?"

"She doesn't know yet. Go get the newspaper, Gerald," Mia called down from the landing.

When he went to retrieve it from his office, Mia peered over the railing. Narrowing her puffy eyes she said, "He never does anything around here. I don't want to be around him tonight. Why don't the two of you go?"

"That's crazy. Just calm down and let's pick a movie," I whispered. Nearby Gerald's footsteps creaked on the oak plank floors.

"I don't care if he hears us," her voice rose. "He's so selfish!"

A knot in my stomach tightened. I sat on the couch and wished I were home eating a squishy glazed jelly donut instead of hearing their constant bickering. Gerald reappeared clutching the newspaper tightly in his fist. He flopped down next to me and squinted at the show-time listings.

"Mia, do you think you can finish getting ready in the next half hour?" he asked.

"I *am* ready. Don't I look ready?" she said, sweeping down the staircase like Scarlett O'Hara.

"Yes, you look ready, but I'll bet money you're not ready to walk out the door, right?

"The minute we step outside, my hair's going to frizz. What are you so upset about? We haven't even picked a movie yet, *dear*." Mia inspected herself in the living room mirror.

I wanted to leave, but that would have made Mia even angrier. "Look, if the two of you would rather do something else tonight, that'd be okay with me," I said, trying to simplify the situation.

"Foreign films are out because Gerald won't read subtitles. He only wants action flicks. How's that for sophistication?"

"Oh, so now you're a sophisticate? I'll have you know I'm not used to my new graduated bifocals, and it's hard to focus with the words at the bottom of the screen and the people at the top," he volleyed.

"You just can't read fast enough." She sank into the easy chair next to the couch.

I leaned back and closed my eyes to escape, remembering how foreign movies used to be my favorites. I would catch all of the European films at the Garden Hills Cinema on Peachtree Road with my old boyfriend, Alejandro. Afterward we would usually grab a slice of pizza at Fellini's and discuss the screening.

He always held Hollywood films in contempt and said, "American directors are caught up in the star system. Their movies lack realism—Jack Nicholson is always Jack Nicholson."

"Yes, I'd much rather see a film where you're not distracted by the star's personality."

"Rochelle, that is exactly how I feel."

The way he rolled the *R* in my name made it seem sexy and mysterious. "Rochelle" had always sounded like someone who should be playing bridge with my mother.

Gerald swiped at the table with the newspaper. I opened my eyes and saw Mia and him staring at me.

"So what haven't you seen yet?" Mia turned to me.

"I'd love a sexy thriller. I heard there's a new one out."

"I would be a thrilled if we had any sex in this house," she said, smoothing her hair and delivering the line with a swagger like Mae West.

I picked up the first magazine I could grab from the coffee table. Flipping through the pages of a dermatology journal, I stared at inflamed bull's-eye-shaped welts in an article about how to recognize Lyme disease.

When Alejandro and I had gone hiking in the north Georgia mountains, I felt we were like the two lovers in the classic French movie, *A Man and a Woman*—two people running in slow motion toward each other and landing in a passionate embrace in a grassy field. He had said, "You really should come with me to

Madrid one day. You would love the Retiro Park with all its beautiful walking trails."

"I'd love to, but I'd better start saving my money," I said, scratching my leg, wondering if the bites I was feeling were from the Lyme ticks I had heard about in a warning on National Public Radio. I was hoping they were just mosquitoes. That was before I knew about the West Nile virus. It was a day I'll never forget.

Alejandro said, "Rochelle, I think we should date only each other. What do you think?"

"I think this makes us official." I said, pulling him down beside me on the grass.

Through clinched teeth Gerald muttered, "I guess we'd better forget about seeing a Woody Allen film. I get enough talky, neurotic women at home."

"Yeah, and I've just about had my fill of watching a short loser who whines all the time."

I put down the magazine and said, "Okay, it's time to break it up and go to your separate corners. We're just trying to agree on a movie—is it so impossible? I'm going to get something to drink in the kitchen and hopefully the two of you will work it out by the time I get back."

I walked down the hall, passing by their framed wedding portrait. The couple smiled blissfully for the camera. Mia and Gerald had recently remodeled their kitchen, but they had retained the original style of the house. Leaded windows in the wooden cabinets revealed colorful vintage dishes and kitsch souvenir glassware from various states. I poured ice water into a tumbler imprinted with illustrations of Stone Mountain and the Georgia State Capitol. A gleaming brass espresso machine was nestled into a niche in the corner. The weather was too hot for me to want to drink coffee.

Over cups of cappuccino, Alejandro had explained his take on the updated film version of *Carmen* we had seen. He had said the Spanish director Carlos Saura had explored flamenco as a metaphor for love and betrayal. *Carmen* was a story within a story, interspersing the private lives of the actors with their roles in a flamenco performance. I knew that Saura's wife, the American actress Geraldine Chaplin, was completely bilingual, but she had said on a talk show that she still dreams in English. I had started taking adult-education Spanish lessons. My mind raced ahead to my future with Alejandro.

Gerald glanced at his watch and exhaled with a snort. "Rochelle, soon it's not going to matter what we decide because it's getting late, and mall traffic is a bear if we're going to the movies at North Point. At this rate we probably won't be able to make the eight o'clock shows, and ten o'clock is out because I've got early morning patients tomorrow. I need to get some sleep tonight."

"Did I ever warn you not to marry a doctor?" Mia asked. She grabbed the movie section and ran her long nails down the columns. "Doctors are so predictable."

"I'm not big on surprises," I said.

I had given up on surprises ever since I had decided to drop by Alejandro's apartment one Saturday morning. I had run by the donut shop to pick up some French crullers and two cups of steaming coffee. Carefully balancing the bag on the seat next to me, I headed for his place in Midtown. I walked down the hallway to his door and tried the handle. It moved freely, so I stuck my head inside and called out, "*Buenos días, mi amor.*"

"I'll be out in a minute, Rochelle. Don't come in! *Un momentito.*"

I was already standing in the living room and had a clear view of his bedroom. Alejandro was scrambling to put on his shorts, and I saw the triumphant look of the woman who was sitting in bed clutching the sheets to her breasts. I dropped the bag, splattering coffee on the rug and all over my shoes. I groped for the door and darted down the hallway.

Mia stood up and placed her arms akimbo. "I've made a decision. We're going to see that new mystery with Denzel where he's a bad guy—a killer."

"I've already seen it, and I was shocked that the sister's the assassin," I blurted out.

"Now I won't need to go. Thanks a lot for spoiling it for me. The two of you are always ganging up on me." Mia's lower lip jutted forward. "Gerald never wants to do what I want and you're just as bad."

"Me?" Gerald shouted, aiming his finger at my sister. "You're the one who can't make a decision. And when you do, it's always something that suits only you. You're the most selfish person I've ever met."

Mia moved closer, almost spitting in Gerald's face with her words. "The last time I wanted to go to Fratelli's for dinner, you said you didn't want Italian. We ate barbecue ribs instead. Remember?" her voice cracked.

Their insults flew back and forth. Mia yelled, "What about that dinner with the pharmaceutical rep two months ago? Think I really enjoyed hearing about zits and carbuncles while I was eating?"

"All those zits and carbuncles, as you put it, pay for this house, our movies, *and* our dinners." Gerald glared at Mia with sparks in his eyes.

I wrapped the strap of my purse around my wrist and pulled myself up from the deep crevice in the overstuffed couch. I'd had enough—too much talk, too many thoughts of Alejandro, and a gnawing sweet tooth was calling to me. I quietly lurched forward and turned the knob on the front door. Maybe the "hot light" was still lit.

Of Wheelchairs and Wings:
The Michelle Donovan Story

By George Weinstein

Michelle Donovan passed out cold on the first day of her first teaching job. Classes at Parklane Elementary in East Point didn't start until the next week, but panic had already set in. Her assistant Debra revived her, and Michelle, still lightheaded and perspiring, looked at her class list again. Though she would be teaching just five students, they all had polio, cerebral palsy, or sickle-cell anemia, along with two cases of congenital heart disease. She had completed a teaching degree in special education at West Georgia College in the spring, but for kids with orthopedic impairments and medical issues she needed an entirely different set of skills.

Debra appeared to size her up from across the desk and Michelle saw herself through this experienced woman's eyes. With her overalls and long hair up in a ponytail, Michelle knew she looked about fifteen. She could read Debra's thoughts: *They gave me a baby to take care of.*

Instead, Debra said, "You okay? You need some water?"

"I'm fine, thanks. I guess it hit me all at once. I've worked with some children in wheelchairs, but this is way out of my field."

"They're good kids. You'll end up knowing more about what's going on inside them than their doctors do. Shoot, after a year of this you might decide to go to medical school."

"No, I have a problem with blood."

"You faint?"

Michelle smiled. "Good guess."

Debra made lots of good guesses about her that first year. She noticed Michelle's tendency to focus on a particular child and would call out, "Hey, what's TJ doing over there?" to broaden her perceptions. She taught her to be aware of the whole classroom at all times. A fourth-generation teacher, Michelle loved the children and the atmosphere of the classroom, but Debra helped her discover a love for the work itself.

Toward the end of the school year, Michelle pointed that out to Debra. "You ever teach a kid to ride a bike?"

"Yeah, a few."

"That's what you did for me. After a while, I didn't even notice your hands on my back. One day I looked over my shoulder and you were way behind, waving and clapping. I knew I could do this."

"Just don't fall and cut your knee. I'd hate to see you faint again."

For the next three years, Michelle taught all day and went to night school at Georgia State to get a Master's in orthopedic impairment. The work took every bit of her effort and creativity, but she found she'd made the perfect choice for her interests. She could take back to the classroom everything she learned about wheelchairs and walkers as well as anatomy and therapies. Michelle was hooked.

As medical technology advanced, children with ever greater needs could attend school. Kyle was five years old when he came to Michelle's class at Mimosa Elementary in Roswell. He had lung disease, and a tracheotomy helped him breathe, but he still needed to be on oxygen during the day and a ventilator at night. His skin always looked dusky blue. Kyle had to be suctioned too, and he required a feeding tube—it seemed that nothing was right. Yet, Kyle smiled all the time.

Michelle had grown up as one of the original Trekkies, and one of the first questions she always asked her new students was, "Do you like *Star Trek?*" Kyle couldn't talk much, but she saw it in his eyes and the extra-wide grin: he loved *Star Trek.* She rewarded his progress with *Star Trek* stickers on a motivational behavior chart, even getting him to eat a little bit on his own.

All of the "normal" kids accepted Kyle immediately. Michelle was pushing one of her children back from the lunchroom one day, and they nearly collided with a five-year-old from a regular kindergarten class pulling the smiling Kyle down the hall in a wagon. For the two years he attended Michelle's class, his sunny nature touched everyone at Mimosa.

Michelle knew that Kyle lived on borrowed time, but she tried not to think about it. After she visited him in the hospital on one occasion, she fantasized about him being touched by an angel and dashing from the medical building under his own power, his cheeks rosy as he ran so fast that no child could keep up. For children with physical impairments, however, even the smallest, shortest-lived steps can be miraculous—just breathing on their own for a time or mastering one part of their bodies.

One Sunday, Kyle's nurse called Michelle to say that he had died. His classmates got the adults through the days that followed. On Monday, one of Michelle's students said, "Oh, Kyle is in heaven, running around, and he's having such a good time." The children talked among themselves, speculating about the games Kyle played in heaven that his impairments had prevented here. They brought in toy telephones and called him up and talked to him during the school day.

Kyle's father, Karl, spoke at the funeral. A week or so before he passed away, Kyle had wanted to make something for his father's birthday. Michelle's longtime assistant Carole helped him as he wrote on pieces of paper all the things he planned to do for his dad, applying himself as never before. Carole bound the pages together and sent them home with him, in time for the birthday party. Karl talked about how much that gift meant to him, reinforcing Michelle's feeling that the things the kids grew especially excited about doing could foster the most learning and bring the most joy. Everyone learned from Kyle as well. Michelle often remembered the miracle of his smile and imagined him as free as a bird, his face and body radiant.

Sometimes, miracles flew in on the most surprising wings. Michelle couldn't have predicted such a thing when a boy named Justin enrolled in her class. He had cerebral palsy; as a quadriplegic, he spent his days confined to a wheelchair, unable to move very much. Justin didn't communicate orally, but could point to symbols. She asked him to show her a dog and he gestured at the correct picture right away.

Kyle and all of Michelle's other kids gave her daily inspiration—and a few of them provided momentary exasperation—but the nonverbal children resonated deepest with her. Justin talked with his eyes and his hands, and Michelle paid attention and listened. She worked with Justin until he could string symbols together to make sentences.

When the Gulf War broke out in 1991, she wanted her class to write to somebody stationed over in the Middle East. In addition to demonstrating their patriotism, her class could work on grammar, social studies, and current events.

"Can we ask them anything we want?" one of her boys said, rubbing his hands together.

"Anything."

"Can we ask if they, like, killed somebody?"

"Just make sure you use good sentence structure."

This assignment appealed to every one of the children. They all typed on computers in their different ways, some trotting out their most bloodthirsty questions, but others asking their most poignant ones: "Do you have boys and girls back home? Can we write to them and say hello for you?" Justin pointed to the things he wanted to say, and Michelle wrote them down alongside the others' work.

They sent the letter with a class picture to the Navy Department. Two months later, an F-14 pilot on the carrier *Independence* named Captain Jay Yakeley wrote back that he shared their letter with the whole ship. The class began a correspondence with their new friend, the decorated naval aviator who used the call sign "Spook." From his jet, Spook shot videos of camels in the desert, oil fields, and takeoffs and landings on the carrier. He set the images to music and sent the films to Michelle's class.

They replied with videos of class projects. The boys at play pretended to be Captain "Spook" Yakeley instead of Captain Kirk. As Christmas neared, the class sent t-shirts with the children's handprints and a video of them singing carols.

The following February, Michelle got a phone call at the school. "This is Jay Yakeley," the caller said. She'd never heard his voice before. He told her, "We're back in California. How do you think the kids would like it if I flew my F-14 out to Dobbins Air Reserve Base, so they could see it and meet me and my navigator?"

"Like it?" she said. "As soon as I tell them, you'll be able to hear their cheering all the way over in San Diego."

They set a date and her class got busy. They made a big box of Southern souvenirs, with postcards, Moon Pies, pecans, and peanuts, and put in lots of class pictures. On the day of Jay's arrival, everyone dressed in red, white, and blue. Michelle, Carole, and the other assistants decorated the wheelchairs with crepe paper, and they led a convoy of kids and parents from Roswell to Dobbins.

When "Spook" carried each child up the ladder to look in the cockpit, he said, "See, we're strapped in just like you are in your wheelchair. We have to do our best all the time and stay focused." The kids loved it, pointing and asking questions. Justin only pointed, of course, but Jay explained everything he could.

After everyone had a turn up top, Jay and his navigator showed the children and their parents the underside of the plane, the wheels, and places for armaments. Justin must have been sitting too far away, because he leaned forward, straining to hear and see more. Michelle was pointing her camcorder at him as he gripped his wheels. For the first time in his life, he pushed his wheelchair. She got it on video, though her hands trembled and her eyes burned.

Michelle rushed over and said, "Justin, I am so, so proud of you!" He smiled and smiled for the camera, obviously pleased with himself.

She continued to praise him, crying, "I cannot believe you did it!"

Justin looked at her and laughed. As clear as day, he said, "Spook."

Who could hold back the tears over this miracle? Jay and his navigator, tough, battle-hardened veterans, wept at least as much as Michelle and the others.

For many of Michelle's kids, such success leads to exciting new possibilities: Justin left her after seven years and went on to graduate from Roswell High School. Twenty-five years of teaching children with orthopedic impairments—more than half her lifetime and far longer than anyone else in Fulton County—has allowed her to give the best part of herself. And seeing her children push open doors of opportunity on their own provides Michelle with rewards that none of her many teaching honors can match. To witness Justin in action, to remember Kyle's smile—that's as good as it gets.

Mind Your Language

By Terry Baddoo

"Pomeranian. Listen. Pom-er-rain-eyan. Again, after me. Pom."

"Palm."

"No, not 'palm,' Pom. As in pom-pom."

"Pom."

"Better. Pom-er."

"Pom-er."

"Rain-eyan."

"Ran-eyan."

"No, rain,rain. Pom-er-rain-eyan. Come on, you're not trying."

"I am. I am trying. I just don't want to do this."

"Of course you do. You're just nervous that's all."

"Dad, I'm not nervous. I just don't care, okay. It's crap."

"Hey! Mind your language."

"That's all I ever do."

"Don't be cute."

"Well it's true."

"Look, we've talked about this, haven't we?"

"No, you and Mom have talked about it. It's all I ever get:—Articulate. Resonate. Elucidate. I'm sick of it. I hate public speaking."

"Don't be silly."

"I do. I hate it. It's embarrassing."

"But you've always loved to compete."

"When I was a kid, maybe, but—"

"But now you're full grown man of fourteen, it's beneath you, right?"

"No, but it's just—"

"You're odds-on for the gold."

"I don't care about the gold. That's your dream, not mine."

"That's not fair. We're all in this together. We're a team."

"A team? It's the Fulton County Oratory Contest, not the Olympics."

"It's a family tradition."

"Well, I'm starting a new one. Private speaking. I'll just mumble to myself."

"Now you're being childish."

"But Dad, why can't we be normal? Like Michael's family. They go to football games on Saturdays. Georgia Bulldogs. Got season tickets and everything. And look at Kerry Patterson."

"Who?"

"You know, the girl with braces? Two doors down…you spoke at her uncle's firm last Christmas."

"Oh, yes. BellSouth, wasn't it?"

"I don't know…anyway, her family goes to Destin every year. Third week in June. All of them, including her cousins. They have a great time. Now that's a family tradition. Not elocution parties."

"They're very popular."

"To you and your friends, maybe, not to me. Come as your favorite sibilant, what's that all about? It's ludicrous."

"Good diction gets you a lot further than football and seaside holidays, young man."

"But people don't speak like us. It's phony. 'The Pomeranian's cranium was found in the geraniums.' What does that mean? It's nonsense."

"It's not supposed to mean anything. It just shows the judges you can enunciate."

"But I thought you said speech was about communication?"

"It is."

"Then what's the point of talking gibberish just because it sounds good?"

"Listen, I explained this already. It's verbal gymnastics. Think of it as an exercise. It shows off your breathing, your vowels, your consonants. It just proves you're in control of what you're saying."

"But I'm not."

"Not what?"

"Not in control of what I'm saying. You wrote it. I just mouth the words. I'm like…what's that puppet called?"

"I don't know what you're talking about."

"Toby the Tiger. That's it. I'm Toby the Tiger. And you're Johnny Fortune."

"Who?"

"Johnny Fortune. You know, "It's Toby Time with Johnny Fortune.""

"The ventriloquist? Now you're being ridiculous."

"Well, what's the difference?"

"Look, Jason, public speaking is an art. You can't compare it with some cheesy variety act."

"So why do all the kids think I'm weird?"

"I'm sure they don't."

"They do. They say I'm poncy and weird."

"Poncy?"

"Oh, you know, it's like what you said about Mrs. Jacobs that time."

"What? Jenny Jacobs?"

"How many Mrs. Jacobs do you know?"

"Well, there's older and younger actually, but go on."

"Well, you know when she directed you in that play? The one you did at the hospice."

"Major Barbara?"

"Whatever. Anyway, she started calling everyone 'darling' and 'luvvie', remember?"

"Vaguely."

"And you didn't like it, did you? You said she was pretentious."

"So?"

"So, that's what they mean—pretentious, poncy. And that's what they call me at school."

"Oh, that's just ignorance."

"Is it? Or are they just unusually perceptive?"

"They're riffraff that's all. Philistines."

"Maybe. But it doesn't help me much, does it? They still trash my locker and call me faggot. How would you like it? They think I'm a freak."

"Look, you can't go around worrying what other people think all the time. So what if you are different? Different is good. I mean, nothing changes if everyone stays the same, does it? You've just got to be true to yourself."

"But I'm not being true to myself, am I? I'm being true to you. If I was being true to myself, I might fit in and I wouldn't be such a loser."

"So that's what this is all about."

"What?"

"Fitting in."

"No. Well, yes. I mean…oh, I don't know."

"Look, Jason, if you're having trouble at school, you should have told me."

"I am telling you."

"Well, that may be, but now's not the time. We'll talk about it later, okay? So come on, wet those chords, you're on in five minutes."

"Oh, I give up…POMERANIAN!"

The Gravity Game

By Terry Segal

We used to play The Gravity Game with our babies when they learned to grasp and hold objects. They discovered that when they dropped them, we picked them up. The rules were simple. Things that drop get picked up.

Our babies grew and, as it turns out, there is an adult version of The Gravity Game. It's not as much fun as the other one. Its rules are cruel. Things drop and they don't get picked up without the aid of a plastic surgeon.

Who knew that I had a reserve set of eyelids waiting just underneath my eyebrows to be released on my fiftieth birthday like front seat air bags?

How is it that my perky breasts, those that with the aid of some miraculous bra could inflate to be used as chin rests, have dropped like the ball on New Year's Eve?

Fifty years of sitting on my rear end must have weakened the elastic. I have to watch that my buns don't get tucked into the back of my knee socks when I pull them up. I've realized that that's the reason little old people walk the way they do.

That extra tent flap of Expando-skin that stretched out front to house my babies can now effectively be used as a spare Hide-a-Key.

Regardless of the climate, I wear a scarf around my neck through the month of November, lest I get mistaken for a turkey and served up at someone's feast.

My jawbone has developed little pillows, in case I should want to coquettishly roll my head to the side, midday, to drool and snore.

Even my spirits sag! But that's okay. I told my husband that playing this version of The Gravity Game keeps me from only being admired as a sex goddess and affords me the opportunity to work on my personality.

Random Thoughts

By John Sheffield

Armor Has Its Weaknesses

I once worked with a man in a company in Alpharetta who was a great manager and a truly decent person. His only weakness was a penchant for malapropisms. I think he knew that speaking was not his forte, but his solution for dealing with this problem was unfortunate. He learned complex words and interesting phrases that he then mangled. A notable example occurred when we were discussing a problem with a scientist at another laboratory.

"Are you sure he's trying to screw us?" I asked.

"Yes. He keeps trying to hire key people away. He reckons their funding will go with them."

"Is there anything we can do?"

"He thinks I can't do anything but I think I've found a chintz in his armor."

Chintz? My memory of chintz was of the fabric on my great aunt Lily's sofa and easy chairs. An image rapidly formed in my mind of the evil scientist clad in gaudy, floral-patterned underwear. "I think you're onto something," I replied.

Salesmen: Intimidation, Envy, and Victory

Our curious python, Cynthia, was sunning herself on the tall lamp by the sofa when the persistent encyclopedia salesman from Marietta came to our house. I ushered him to the sofa. Cynthia's head edged forward sinuously. The salesman knew he was being watched—but by whom? When Cynthia's tongue was about to flick his ear, he turned.

"Hell!" he said, as he bolted for the door.

Cynthia's best friend is our elderly dog George. One summer evening, we were having drinks on the patio with my cousin, Bert, a car salesman. George was engaged in his favorite pastime—licking his private parts. Cynthia and Bert were studying the dog intently.

"I wish I could do that," said Bert enviously.

"Yes, but would George approve of it?" my wife retorted.

George barked, signaling a visitor.

"Our vacuum cleaner can beat yours," the salesman said.

"Let's see," I replied.

I vacuumed the carpet.

After re-vacuuming, he showed me the additional dirt collected.

I repeated the process showing what he had missed.

Cynthia eyed the vacuum hose as it followed him through the door, then retired to the lamp—pleased that another enemy had been defeated.

Alpharetta International

The rail link in Atlanta airport circles around between the baggage area and terminals T, A, B, C, D, and E. To help passengers, a voice announces arrival at terminal T as in tango, A as in alpha and so on. I assume this is mainly for the benefit of non-English-speaking peoples. Every time I hear these announcements I am reminded of Lily Tomlin's wonderful act as a telephone operator with nasally spoken lines such as, "Is this the party to whom I am speaking?" and wonder what she would do as the announcer on the rail link in the mythical international airport in Alpharetta with its terminals A, E, G, K, P, and R.

"The train has arrived at E as in euphoric."

"Those traveling to Augusta, please dismount at terminal G as in gnome."

"The next terminal is K as in knee."

She would carefully enunciate terminal P as in psychology.

For the benefit of the Japanese, there would be terminal R as in legal.

I invite you to make up your own confusions, not forgetting A as in aardvark.

I have another thought, not about airports, but about alphabets. French does not have a 'w' in its alphabet. The *double-vey*, as they call it, only appears in foreign words like *wagons lits*. Just think about what they are missing. Why worry whether warriors want wealth when women will win with wonderful words.

Biographies

Terry Baddoo is a British journalist who came to Atlanta in 1995. He's been charged by an elephant in Kenya; chased by soccer hooligans in Sweden; nearly drowned in New Zealand; threatened by knife-wielding gypsies in Greece; and tear-gassed in England. He's covered the fall of the Berlin Wall; the end of apartheid in South Africa; four FIFA World Cups; three Summer Olympics; and can thank Pete Sampras, among others, for the fact that he now resides in the USA. And he puts all this down to writing.

Buzz Bernard, a native Oregonian, lives in Roswell with his German-born wife and Chinese dog. He—Buzz, not the dog—is the author of five nonfiction books, but now concentrates on writing novels and short stories. He's a charter member of the Alpharetta Barnes and Noble Writers Workshop.

British-born *Cecilia Branhut* moved over 30 years ago, on a whim, from London to New York City. She'd enjoyed a brief career in the theatre in England, but fell into advertising in New York. Marriage took her to Detroit, divorce and a promotion took her to Atlanta, and writing accompanied her along the way…as a copywriter, editor and sometime journalist. Cecilia now proudly boasts dual British-American citizenship, is a serene Alpharetta resident, and is retired from corporate America. She wishes she were a more organized and less procrastinating writer.

Michael Buchanan, raised in Atlanta, presently lives in Alpharetta. A high school teacher for thirty years, he has been recognized for his classroom creativity by *USA Today*, the *Atlanta Journal Constitution* and by his peers as Teacher-of-the-Year in 2001. Buchanan co-authored the novel *Micah's Child* with Diane Lang. He has been published in the anthology *O Georgia!*, and has written articles for artifact magazines and for the Georgia Council of Math Teachers. Lang and Buchanan have finished their second novel, *Cry of the Quetzal*, and a biography about an obese teenager, *Please Don't Read This Page, The Fat Boy Chronicles*. A regular speaker on Celebrity Cruises, he speaks throughout the South to book clubs and educational groups. His interests include diving for artifacts and fossils in Southeastern rivers as well as reef diving in the Caribbean.

Paul Bussard retired from a forty-year career in data processing (aerospace and communication) and is busier than ever with his writing, gardening and woodworking. He is an avid reader and writer of science fiction, but dabbles in poetry and human interest stories. He and his wife, Patty, recently moved from North Georgia to Texas to be near their growing grandchildren. Paul is VP of the Woodlands Writers Guild, a member of Writers in the Hat, and participates in the Northpoint Barnes & Noble writers' group via e-mail and phone.

Kathleen Craft Boehmig loves to write about her southern heritage. She, husband Paul and "two Allens" (her father and her son), all native Atlantans, live in Roswell. They share their household with a laid-back golden retriever who ignores Kathleen's parakeet and lives in fear of her cranky Senegal parrot. Kathleen has written feature pieces for local periodicals, but her focus is short memoir-style essays, several of which have been published in *O, Georgia!, Lessons Learned, Sacred Stones*, and *Chicken Soup for the Grandma's Soul*. She is working on a book of essays, serves on the board of The Atlanta Writers Club, is a member of the prestigious "Elements" critique group, and is deeply appreciative of the Barnes & Noble Alpharetta Writers Workshop.

Brooks Dumas wrote and illustrated her first book when she was six. For a time she aspired to be a dancer like her famous cousin Ann Miller, but her parents encouraged her to go to college and become an educator. Recently she passed the torch to the next generation of teachers, so she can finally concentrate on writing poems, short stories, and family stories which reflect the uniqueness of the Southern experience. Her writing is inspired by her father and her husband who, she says, could both be characters in a novel. She is currently compiling stories about her childhood, living in the manager's quarters of an old Florida motel. Although her husband tells her to "hurry and write a Dan Brownbuster," Brooks is savoring the discovery process of doing research, finding her voice, and growing as a writer. Brooks and her husband Steve live in Alpharetta near their two grown children, Stephanie and Brent.

Rob Elliott is the founding member of the North Point Writers Workshop. Besides working on historical fiction, he can be found hoofing it through the dust of Civil War reenactment battlefields across the South. He currently lives in Pembroke, Georgia where he teaches High School English.

Ann Foskey hails from Woodstock, Georgia where she gets her kicks watching wild turkey disappear—the feathered kind, that is—the ones that wander through her neighborhood and occasionally stop traffic on Wiley Bridge Road. When she is not visiting Ossabaw Island, the setting of her first book, or at her computer writing poetry and prose about the wilds of Georgia for "Still Small Voices," her second book, she can be spotted along highway 92—idling in coffee shops, Kohls, or the carpool line—sometimes with a wild turkey feather in her hair.

Bobbi Kornblit is passionate about the written word. The author, journalist and writing coach holds a Master of Art in Professional Writing from Kennesaw State University. Her short stories and poetry have appeared in several anthologies including *Lessons Learned* and *O' Georgia! A Collection of Georgia's Newest and Most Promising Writers.* Her debut novel is currently with an agent who is in search of a publisher. Bobbi covers the fun side of life—the arts, food and travel for local and national publications. She teaches a grammar course at Emory's Professional Learning Program. In 1994 she and her husband, Simon, moved to Sandy Springs from Los Angeles after being tossed around in the Northridge quake.

Walter Lawrence grew up with a love for words and became a poet at a young age. He was recently published in the *Chattahoochee Review,* the *O Georgia* anthology, and in several regional magazines.

Dagmar Marshall received her Associate of Arts Degree in Journalism from Green Mountain College, VT. A Northeasterner by birth, a Southerner by choice, Dagmar and her family have been residents of Georgia since 1963. Dagmar spent twenty-five years in Real Estate in the Atlanta area, was a Managing Broker and had her own Marketing Business for Agents. She is the proud Mom of three and proud Grandmom of five. Retiring from Real Estate meant putting writing first—at last. Dagmar's first novel, "The Closing" was published in November, 2005. She has had several short-stories appear in the "O'Georgia" and "American Review" Anthologies.

Judy Parker-Matz is a liberated, California, 1960's brat who migrated to the Northern Atlanta suburbs in 1995. She is a new member of the Barnes & Noble writing group and is beginning the journey of writing her memoir about the strong, courageous and colorful women who make up her Armenian family lineage. Educated with a bachelor's degree in communications and her MBA, Judy's day job consists of working for a Pittsburgh-based consulting firm, designing and implementing large, enterprise-wide computer-system training programs. She lives in a lake-front home in Cumming with her aging mother, two yellow, male tabby cats and loves being surrounded by the North Georgia woods and wildlife.

Carolyn Robbins currently lives in Marietta, Georgia with her husband and her cat, Simba. She's been writing for the amusement of her children for years. Now that they are grown, she's published a novel, *Caribbean Green,* and a magazine article.

Jordan Segal is a fifteen-year old honors student at Roswell High School. He speaks English and French and can read Hebrew. He's interested in a career as a film director. In his free time, he enjoys playing basketball, Hackysack, Ultimate Frisbee and break-dancing. He's the middle child, having both an older and younger sister. He resides with his family in Roswell, GA.

Terry Segal is a licensed Marriage & Family Therapist in Roswell, Georgia. She has a Ph.D. in Energy Medicine from Greenwich University, a Master of Arts degree in Educational Psychology from California State University-Northridge, and a Master of Arts degree in Theatre from the University of Miami in Florida. She uses the arts to heal the soul. She has just completed a novel, *The Corners of Me That Are Mine*, and has also written a play version. If her son, Jordan, makes it as a film director, she will write and star in the screenplay as well. In the meantime, she is writing a self-help book, *The Enchanted Journey: Finding the Key That Unlocks You.* Terry enjoyed an earlier career as a model, dancer, and actress before becoming a producer—of three children. She and her husband Fred, and family, reside in Roswell, GA.

John Sheffield is a semi-retired physicist from England who has pursued the dream of fusion energy since the late 1950s, and has published widely on fusion, energy in general, and the environment. Including his childhood near London, he has been bombed in more than one sense of the word. He lives in Roswell with his Latvian-Australian wife, Dace. They have two Texan children, and a cat, Calvin, who has refined the art of complaining over his fourteen years with them.

Marre Dangar Stevens is a daughter of a family native to Georgia from before the trail of tears. She has a husband, a son and a garden. She writes, cooks and gardens.

George Weinstein writes novels and short stories, and lives with his wife Katherine and their two furry children, Ruby and Angie, in Roswell. George is president of the Atlanta Writers Club (www.atlantawritersclub.com) and participates in the North Point Barnes & Noble writers group.

Contributors and Contributions

Terry Baddoo: An Afternoon Off
Mind Your Language

Buzz Bernard: Beaner
Great Skin-So-Soft Soapy Butt Caper

Cecilia Branhut: A Good Idea—But Whose?
Red in the Post Office

Michael Buchanan: The Choice

Paul A. Bussard: Obrero
Pantoum of Truth

Kathleen Craft Boehmig: May's Biscuits
Song of the Mockingbird
Tree Bark and Tadpoles

Brooks Dumas: Chocolate Deception
Coat of Many Colors

Rob Elliott: Crossing the Chattahoochee

Ann Foskey: A Room without a View
McFarland Road

Bobbi Kornblit: Pick a Flick

Walter Lawrence: The Bargain King
The Package

Dodge Lewis: Joe

Dagmar Marshall: Bozo, Dog Of The 'Hood

Judy Parker-Matz:	A Southern California Brat Migrates to Georgia
Carolyn Robbins:	Fishing Indoors Learning to Live Together
Jordan Segal:	Literary Lines High School Graduation
Terry Segal:	The Mammogram Follow-up Mammogram His World, The Gravity Game The Recital, Free How to Live When You're Away From Me
John Sheffield:	Alien Roswell Any Questions, Master Gardeners? Chinese Zodiac Random Thoughts
Marre Dangar Stevens:	Humming Bird Call I Learned Two Deaths Today
George Weinstein:	Of Wheelchairs and Wings: The Michelle Donovan Story The Gaffe of the Magi Elfscapade

978-0-595-41535-9
0-595-41535-0

Printed in the United States
141978LV00004B/79/A

9 780595 415359